THE BAD STEP

First edition published by Pennine Pens in e-book format 2014
This edition published in 2016 by
Gritstone Publishing Co-operative
Birchcliffe Centre
Hebden Bridge
HX7 8DG
http://gritstone.coop

Gritstone Publishing Co-operative is jointly owned by its members, some of
Britain's best-regarded authors writing about the countryside and the outdoors.
Look out for our other titles.

© Andrew Bibby 2014, 2016
Typeset by Carnegie Book Production, Lancaster
Printed by Jellyfish Solutions Ltd
Cover photo © Steve Pipe, cumbrianrambler.blogspot.co.uk

ISBN 978-0-9955609-0-1

Catalogue in publication data is available from the British Library.

The author is choosing to make a contribution of 45p, representing 5% of
this book's cover price, for each book sold to the Langdale and Ambleside
Mountain Rescue Team.

THE BAD STEP

by Andrew Bibby

GRITSTONE
PUBLISHING

Prelude

The first edition of the next day's Daily Telegraph was going to press in five minutes. It gave Jill Nicholson, working a freelance sub-editing shift on the sports pages, about three minutes to re-jig the bottom of page 23. Inter Milan had signed a mid-field player from Roma, not earth-shattering news, but the Telegraph prided itself on the breadth of its sports coverage and the Italian Serie A had its fair share of British fans. The story had come in late but was already written up: one column, twelve lines of text, single-deck headline.

Jill was looking for another story, roughly the same length, to sacrifice in its place. She had already considered and rejected a piece on drug-testing in professional cycling and a filler on amateur lacrosse in Cheshire. She was now concentrating on a two paragraph story which had originally come through on the agency wires:

Runner dies

Davie Peters, a former British cross-country junior champion, has died at the age of 27. Peters, for a time considered one of the most promising athletes of his generation, won track and cross-country races whilst still a schoolboy and was a member of the UK junior cross-country team in 2002. He subsequently focused on fell-running in his native Lake District.

Davie was taking part in a race in the Lake District at the time of his death. He is believed to have fallen on rocks.

Jill looked up from her terminal. "A dead athlete called Davie Peters," she asked the room. "Anyone ever heard of him?" None of the other subs working on their own screens looked up, but one shrugged. It was a reply of sorts.

"OK, I'm going to kill this piece," Jill muttered, mainly to herself. She blocked the article and dragged it to a small dustbin icon in the corner of her screen, and Davie Peters, his athletic career, his life and his death, disappeared immediately.

Though Jill Nicholson did not know it, it was the second time in twenty-four hours that Davie Peters had been killed.

Chapter 1

The day had started fine, the sun glinting off the waters of Windermere in the early morning light. But then the clouds rolled in. The weather had steadily been worsening. Nick Potterton shivered under a cold Lakeland drizzle.

The blue and green stripes of his running vest, the performance teeshirt he was wearing beneath it and his running shorts were all rapidly becoming sodden. Some runners, hardier than he, were simply in vest and shorts. Ahead of them lay fourteen miles of mountain running, with several thousand feet of climbing for good measure. Nick knew he would be out on the hills for well over three hours. He looked up at the skies: that time was going to be spent under thick cloud.

Running a Lake District fell race was a strange affair. Most people, Nick knew, would find it an incomprehensible way to spend a Saturday. Usually he loved his sport, but just sometimes he thought the general public might be right. Today could turn out to be one of those days.

He positioned himself in the melée of runners waiting for the race to start. He surprised himself sometimes at how he had improved, in the four years since he'd moved north to the Lakes and first put on a pair of fell-running shoes. Really, given that he'd be fifty later in the year, he wasn't at all a bad runner. On the other hand, he had to admit, he wasn't *that* good.

And there certainly were some good runners out today. The Bowfell race was known as one of the Lakeland classic races, a tough mountain challenge that tested a runner's mental resilience almost as much as their physical fitness. It always attracted a strong field. But this year all the big names from the fell-running world were there. This year, Bowfell had been chosen as the final race in the English fell-running championship, and unusually, everything depended on this one race. Five earlier races had been and gone, October had arrived, and it still wasn't clear who was going to be walking off with the men's prize.

Depending on how fast they managed to run round the ridge of mountains that closes off the top end of the valley of Great Langdale from Eskdale and the Scafell range beyond, any one of three runners could get the points needed to win. Nick saw them standing together in the distance ahead of him, chatting with each other.

There was Jim Henderson, short, wiry, still with a Glasgow accent, who'd learned his running skills on craggy Scottish mountains before moving south a couple of years back for a job in Sheffield. He'd had a great season, unexpectedly winning one of the earlier championship races. Still, he was just 23 and there was a general feeling that his successes would come in a year or two's time.

Basically, it came down to two runners. Steve Miller, tall with a distinctive mop of black hair, had just turned thirty. He was a teacher in a comprehensive somewhere on the outskirts of Leeds, good with the kids by all accounts and popular with the other teachers too. His real love, though, was running, and he had talent for it: one of the very best in England in the art of running up and down mountainsides.

His lanky stride as, apparently without effort, he got up the stiffest ascents were a familiar sight at many Cumbrian events. And yet, for whatever reason, he had never won the English Championship. Second placed last time. Second again the year before. Injured the year before that. There was, it seemed, a jinx about the English Champs he seemed unable to break.

And then there was Davie Peters.

Davie was Lakeland born and bred, still living close to the house in Ambleside where he had been brought up. His dad worked as a self-employed driver with some local haulage companies, his mother had had a range of jobs, from hotel receptionist to café waitress – jobs that may not have paid very well but which, as every local knew, were essential if the wheels of the Cumbrian tourism business were going to keep turning. He had a sister, older than him by two years, whom he'd followed through primary and then secondary school. You got the feeling that his parents had simply turned the two children out on to the fells as soon as they'd been able to walk, letting them explore England's most beautiful landscape to their hearts' content. Certainly, Davie had an astonishing knowledge of his home mountains. He seemed to know every shortcut off the hills, each sheep trod, each old mining track.

His forays on the fells as a child had paid off. At school, he wasn't academic but he quickly demonstrated that he could run. He got the cup (carefully made by his teacher from cooking foil) for the under-6s race at his infant school and thereafter never looked back. He won the 100 metres, 200 metres and long jump at his secondary school, and then discovered cross-country. He rapidly made, in turn, the Cumbrian county team and the British juniors. It wasn't always easy for a teenager, but it brought him rewards. The medals and cups from his cross-country days were in pride of place in the living room of his parents' little Ambleside semi.

But then, after school, it had been more difficult. He'd not gone to college, but had found a series of casual jobs close to home. He'd done his fair share of stints in local bars, managed to pass the driving test necessary to use his father's lorry, and then been taken on as a driver by the local council's highways department, before the cuts had begun to bite and the junior staff had all been given redundancy. About this time Davie found himself an upstairs flat above one of the shops in Ambleside's main street, and got himself a second-hand sofa, some kitchen pots and pans and a double bed. The trips away to cross-country events stopped. Instead, Davie turned all his attention to the athletics sport which was there, waiting for him, on his doorstep.

To be a good fell-runner, you have to do two things well. You have to be able to run up mountains as quickly as you can, and you have to be able to descend fast. Davie certainly had the fitness and the experience for the climbs but his real talent was, without question, the way he came down a mountainside. Davie approached a tough descent with the same insouciance he showed in all his running. He seemed not so much to run down a mountain as to glide effortlessly down it, as fast and surefooted as a mountain hare, dancing over the rocks and boulders which stood in his way. God, he was fast. Watching Davie in full descent in a competitive race was a beautiful sight. He was the only runner who made you feel that this was no longer simply a sport, but something higher, more transcendental, an art-form in its own right. Man and mountain appeared as a single organic unity, welded together.

Davie Peters had something else going for him in his running, too, and that was a ruthless competitiveness. Like all great athletes, he was single-minded in his determination to win. Why bother otherwise? In the close-knit world of fell-running, his attitude sometimes caused the odd critical comment. Unlike Steve Miller who would cheerfully stand

5

a round of drinks with other runners in the pub after a race, Davie was inclined to keep himself to himself. He wasn't standoffish, but there was a toughness to his character that few seemed able to penetrate. He was talented, and you knew that he knew it himself.

Nick Potterton still felt that Davie wasn't really a friend, even though they were both members of the same running club, Coniston and Hawkshead Harriers, and were therefore both wearing the same distinctive running vest. It wasn't just that Nick was almost double Davie's age, or until recently had only been to the Lake District on occasional holidays. Nick's background was almost as different as it could be from Davie's: comfortably middle-class, Upper Second in history from Bristol, masters in journalism at City University, and then (no point denying it) a pretty successful professional career working for several of the British national papers. After college and a short stint in the provincial press, he'd fallen into a plum job at the Sunday Times working for the Insight team – not in the glory days, when the paper had broken the thalidomide story for example, but still, he'd been there for some pretty big scoops. Those were the days when investigative journalism was respected and given resources.

And then the move to the Independent, right at the time in 1986 when it was getting off the ground. That was such an exciting time. Nick loved everything about those early years: the sense of building a serious new newspaper from scratch, the energy around, the great use of photographs, his little desk in the office in City Rd overlooking Bunhill Fields, and – of course – the beautiful woman with the long black hair who sat just across from him at the desk the Spanish newspaper El País ran at that stage in the Independent's offices. Ana. What good times there'd been then.

But he'd got restless. He'd bailed out about the time the Indy had one of its first financial wobbles and had moved to Canary Wharf. A stint at the Observer (it hadn't really worked out), a few years at the Mail (he'd never quite found a home there either), and then on to some corporate PR work for one of the big City agencies, some freelancing. And then... well, then of course, suddenly life had changed. Just like that. Now he lived in the Lake District and spent his spare time shivering in the rain waiting (what on earth was the delay?) for this bloody race to actually start.

He forced himself away from his thoughts which were rapidly turning gloomy. Focus, he told himself, get in the zone. The runners around him had quietened down too, trying to listen to a few last minute instructions which the race organiser was bawling out from the start line. And then at last: Ready. Off you go! The long line of runners began to move forward, like a large animal shaking itself into life, and another year's Bowfell fell race was under way.

The Bowfell race begins in Great Langdale. You start in a straightforward enough way, climbing up from the valley bottom to the quiet waters of Stickle Tarn. Then the race turns to cross wild and empty moorland to Angle Tarn, up from there to the great chunk of mountain that is Esk Pike and then climbing again to the even higher summit of Bowfell, the sixth mountain by height in the Lake District complete with magnificent views in all directions. When the weather is fine, that is. When the cloud is down, this is a mountain to treat with respect.

From Bowfell, the race route carries on along the serrated ridge of mountains known as Crinkle Crags. After the Crinkles, runners can look forward to a fast descent down to waters of Red Tarn, before having to tackle the tough climb up to the final summit, Pike o'Blisco.

But first there's the Bad Step. The well-defined path off the summit of Long Top takes the unwary right to the top of a gully with an overhanging shelf of rock which hides a three-metre high vertical drop. Hill-walkers coming this way for the first time are inclined to recoil in surprise. Do you jump? ... and yet the drop is too high to undertake comfortably, especially if you've stopped to worry about it first. Do you try to find a way down the rock face? ... but there seem surprisingly few potential handholds in the places that would help you. Or do you decide to avoid the Bad Step altogether, looking to make your way down the grassy ledges which run out to the left? Oh yes, it's longer but perhaps, in the circumstances, the safer bet.

This last choice is the one which many runners in the Bowfell race are likely to make, even though it means adding precious seconds to their time. But there are those runners who wouldn't dream of such an alternative. Get a handhold and lever yourself half way down the Bad Step, jump the rest.

Nick Potterton found a place in a little group of runners as the pack began the slow ascent up beside the waters of the Stickle Ghyll stream. The climb up to Stickle Tarn seemed for some reason tougher than usual. Maybe it was the absence of all the tourists who normally swarmed up from the valley to look at the tarn. They'd all been driven off the fellside by the weather.

And, thinking about it, Nick realised that what had seemed like relatively light drizzle as he'd waited for the race start had begun to become distinctly stronger and colder. The view ahead, and behind, had disappeared too. His fellow-runners became ghostly companions, barely visible ahead, barely visible if he turned round behind. Shit, this was going to be a tough race, he suddenly realised.

You absolutely had to depend on the compass. Visibility had shrunk still further, the rain had picked up, and – though he knew that several hundred runners couldn't be far away – Nick could see no-one and hear nothing. He was alone in the whiteness.

Oh, the Lakeland fells could be so beautiful. For the past four years, since he'd moved north from his old home in London's Kentish Town to make a new life for himself in Cumbria, Nick had been on a fabulous journey of discovery, gradually getting to know these mountains which were now on his doorstep. Astonishing but true, he'd never before been up England's highest mountain, Scafell Pike. Now he felt he knew the Scafell plateau well, and Great Gable, Glaramara, Bowfell. He'd explored the mountains beyond Wasdale Head, enjoyed the views to the Solway Firth from Pillar and Steeple. He'd spent days too on the Helvellyn range, walked up from both the Thirlmere and the Ullswater sides. Then there was Fairfield, and the Kentmere fells, and Skiddaw, and the Coniston fells, as well. How could he have reached middle age without knowing that this part of England was quite so beautiful?

A week or two after he'd first found rented accommodation in Ambleside and made the move, he'd gone to one of the town's innumerable outdoor shops and bought a decent pair of walking boots, expensive waterproofs and a proper walker's backpack. The fell-running had come a little later, almost by chance. Back in his London days he'd done some jogging and (at Ana's suggestion) had entered a 10K road race for charity. Ana had also told him to talk to the London Marathon press office and get one of the media places they make available, but life was busy, he was a successful journalist, they'd a daughter to bring up, he didn't need extra pressure in his life.

But here in the Lakes, aged 45 and by himself, he found he needed to meet people. He read in the local paper that the Coniston and

Hawkshead running club welcomed new runners on their weekly Thursday pack runs. They'd taken pity on this Londoner, puffing along behind them. In the weeks that followed, they'd got him equipped with a pair of proper fell-running shoes and had helped him as, gradually, his fitness improved.

And so, sometimes with members of his new club and sometimes just by himself, he discovered the Lakeland mountains in a new way, running light over the fells, skipping past the walkers. It was a fantastic discovery. Oh, the Lakeland fells could be so beautiful.

In good weather.

In bad weather, you needed all the mountain experience you'd accumulated. Nick came out of his reverie and assessed his progress. He was somewhere round the back of Rossett Crag, not precisely lost, but definitely off-route. He stopped momentarily and munched a couple of jelly babies, the fell-runners' traditional snack, and as he did so a loud crack of thunder sounded, close at hand. He'd already seen a couple of lightning flashes. God, an electric storm. This would be one of those races where your finishing time didn't matter at all, you just needed to get round safely.

Two miles or more ahead, Steve Miller had also heard the thunder but had barely changed his stride. The weather didn't bother him. He was confident of his abilities as a mountain runner and confident, too, that he could navigate his way round the race course just with a compass. What did bother him quite significantly was the knowledge that Davie Peters was ahead of him. Realistically, it was going to be tough to pull this race back, what with the Crinkle Crags and Pike o'Blisco descents ahead where Davie would definitely have the edge on him. Once again, it seemed, the elusive English Championships gold medal could be going to somebody else.

The race had started promisingly for Steve. He had pulled ahead of both Davie and Jim Henderson on the climb up Stickle Ghyll and had been first through both of the first two checkpoints. But Davie, he knew, would be delighted at the weather conditions. Davie would have a real opportunity to put his knowledge of these fellsides to good use, finding the short cuts and secret trods without Steve or Jim or any of the other runners being able to see where he'd got to.

So Steve was disappointed but not surprised when he reached the third checkpoint, high up at the mountain shelter at Esk Hause to be told by the race marshals there that he was now in second place. Davie had already gone through, about a minute and a half ahead.

Steve turned south, finding easily the path towards Esk Pike. Ninety seconds' lead... There was still a chance he could do this, he reckoned. He could pull back some time on the climb to the next checkpoint on Bowfell and, if he could be ahead of Davie when he reached the Crinkle Crags summit, just before the Bad Step, he would have a real chance of hanging on to the lead for the rest of the race. Another thunder crack sounded but Steve took no notice. He was desperate to win. He willed himself on.

The weather worsened. In Keswick, Ambleside and Windermere visitors to the Lakes sat in the cafés, watched the rain beat against the windowpanes, took an hour over a cup of tea and a cake. It was a day to be indoors at all costs. The National Park centre beside Windermere recorded one of its busiest days of the Autumn. A steady stream of cars headed back along the A66 and A591, as would-be Lakeland tourists cut their losses and decided to head home early. The day had prematurely turned to evening.

In Great Langdale, most of the tents had gone from the National Trust campsite. The warden, dressed in best NT-issue waterproofs, was out, checking that the beck wasn't going to flood the site. As he rubbed the rain from his eyes, he caught sight of a solitary runner, drenched but smiling, his blue and white vest clinging to his body, haring down the footpath off the hills. The first runner from the Bowfell race was back, having overcome the mountains and overcome the weather. It was Steve. He'd managed it. He'd overtaken Davie Peters in the mist on Bowfell, had been told by the marshal at Crinkle Crags that he was the leading runner, had been the first over Pike o'Blisco. He had taken almost two and a half hours, well outside the course record, but he had done it.

Except that there was no welcoming crowd to cheer him back, no finish funnel of stakes carefully taped together for him to run into, no volunteer there with the timing machine. Steve Miller would be the first and only runner to complete the course. Half an hour earlier, the race organiser had formally declared the race abandoned. The marshals at the Crinkle Crags checkpoint had radioed through. A runner had been found at the foot of the Bad Step. Red-black blood, spilled from his skull, stained his blue and green running vest.

Chapter 2

"Not bad, Nick. But – um boring." The speaker was Molly, standing behind him, squinting down at the screen in front of them in the short-sighted way she had. She didn't hold with glasses. The air in the office was fetid. Breaking all the rules about smoking at work, Molly had a cigarette at her lips, which she was contentedly puffing. Whatever the law said (and however much Nick complained), she intended to carry on smoking, even if she was the last person in Britain to do so.

Molly was a big presence in the small room. She was big-breasted, big round the waist and big round the bottom, and yet you never really thought of her as fat. She knew how to carry her size. She gave the impression of being enormously comfortable in the body she had. She was certainly happy to draw attention to it with the clothes she chose to wear. Below the waist would normally be denim or plain slacks, but above the waist Molly felt herself free to give full scope to all the most vibrant colours in the artist's palette. Sometimes it would be a bright violet blouse, sometimes an orange cardigan, sometimes a short-sleeved shirt in the colours of toothpaste. Today it was a canary-coloured top with red polka dots. Nick had yet to discover the Lakeland emporium which provided her with such treasures.

"Beautifully written, but dull." Molly had a northerner's habit of saying it as she found it. And the aggravating thing was that, actually, Molly was absolutely right. Nick knew he had written a perfectly competent story. It met all the rules of good journalism, had the key information in the opening paragraph, included a couple of appropriate quotes... but yes, it was dull.

The problem was that he hadn't wanted to write it at all. Normally, he rather looked forward to the three days a week when he had agreed to give Molly Everett a hand in the run-up to press day at the *Cumbrian Enquirer*, the weekly paper which had been serving the Lake District area since... well, probably since Wordsworth's first encounter with the daffodils. His role was to sub-edit the articles

11

sent in by the paper's network of local contributors, making sure that they'd got the 'i's and the 'e's the right way round in 'achieve', checking there were two 'c's and two 'm's in 'accommodation', and all the sort of stuff that people nowadays just didn't seem to be able to get right. He'd contribute his own stories, too. He'd agreed to write a regular fell-running report for the back page sports section, for example, mainly as a favour to his own club who rather liked having regular coverage of their activities in the paper.

Of course, as soon as he'd got in that Monday morning Molly had asked him to cover the Bowfell race incident. It was marked down as potentially the front page lead. Nick had tried to demur, but Molly was insistent: he had all the contacts, he'd actually *been* there. It was Nick's completed story that they were now looking at on the screen.

Molly was the editor of the *Cumbrian Enquirer*. In effect, she *was* the *Cumbrian Enquirer*. She had begun working for the paper when she'd first left school and had never left. She had come in as a junior, learned her Teeline shorthand, mugged up on her McNae's Essential Law for Journalists, done her exams, become a senior reporter. Then, twenty years ago when old Ralph Nichols had retired, she'd become editor.

Nick had met her six months or so after he'd moved north from London. They'd been at some arts event in Ambleside. Molly, actually in a dress for once (a bright pink creation), had been standing close by and someone he knew had introduced them. "Ah, Molly, you must meet Nick, he's a journalist too, you'll get on." And the strange thing was that they had. They talked trade gossip. They speculated on who was angling for jobs at the NUJ, the journalists' trade union. They discussed the BBC's move to Salford. Molly talked of a Freedom of Information request she'd had turned down and was taking to the Information Commissioner. Nick talked of a similar case he'd had at the Observer.

They'd agreed to meet again for a drink. Molly had asked him whether he was looking for casual shift-work and Nick had agreed. His friends in London when he'd told them had been astonished. From the Sunday Times to the *Cumbrian Enquirer*, that was quite some career progression they told him. The money was laughable, of course. But Nick had reasons for accepting the work. He was short of company and the book he was supposed to be writing was going very slowly indeed. He'd moved to the Lakes mainly because he wanted at that time to get as far away from Kentish Town and his old London life as possible, but also for more whimsical reasons. He'd persuaded a publisher to give him an advance for a book on the apparent renaissance of nuclear power. *Nuclear Power: Yes Please?* he was calling it. What could be more appropriate than to write it just down the road from Sellafield, Britain's most famous – or should that be infamous – nuclear power complex?

As he got to know Molly, the more he rated her. She knew her community inside-out. Her local contacts were phenomenal. And she was a bloody good journalist. She had that instinctive sense of what made a good story. She knew how to peel away the layers to get to the real news which lay below. Her journalistic antennae had sniffed at Nick's piece on the Bowfell race, and something had told her that he'd missed something crucial.

Perhaps, as he tried to tell her, he was just too close to things to be objective. He was still trying to come to terms with what had happened. Though he hadn't known Davie Peters well, they'd been in the same club, they'd been at club runs and parties together. Davie has been there, just ahead of him at the race start. The man had so much talent, he was such an exceptional athlete, absolutely at the top of his form. How could his life have been snatched away so quickly on just another Saturday afternoon?

At first, Nick had assumed the race had been abandoned because of the weather. He felt cross with the race organiser: fell-runners ran in all weathers, and this wasn't any old fell race, this was the English Championships decider. But back in Great Langdale at the bar of the Old Dungeon Ghyll hotel, it didn't take long for him to realise that he had been wrong. Groups of runners who had taken shelter in the bar were talking together in quiet voices, sharing what they'd heard. The story of what had happened just below the highest summit on the Crinkle Crags gradually became pieced together.

If it had been a bad day to be running it had been an even worse day to be one of the race marshals, stuck for hours on end on a checkpoint on a mountain top. The two marshals who had volunteered to go up to Long Top on the Crinkle Crags, Mick Patterson and his mate Bill Butler, were active members of the local Mountain Rescue team so they knew what to expect, but even so they'd found the conditions unpleasant. There'd been problems too with the radio communications, something to do with the lightning apparently, so they'd been forced to try to get a signal for the mobile phone as a back-up. It meant that Steve Miller almost took them by surprise as he emerged from out of the cloud, pounding the rocky path that led to Long Top and looking strong. Mick was the first to recognise the runner as he approached: "Great running, Steve, keep it up."

Steve nodded and disappeared immediately from the summit, heading in the direction of the Bad Step. Almost straight away a second runner also materialised from out of the weather. "He's just ahead of you, Davie," Mick Patterson had said. "Sixty seconds or so, nothing more than that." Davie Peters acknowledged the comment with a wave of his hand without changing his stride, and like Steve Miller carried on straight down the path.

Then there had been a pause. Five minutes had gone by. Six. The two marshals waited together for the third runner to appear. Seven minutes. Eight. There could be no doubt that this race was now definitely a two-horse affair. And then finally Jim Henderson appeared. Although he was going well, it looked as if he was finding the course a challenge. This was one of those occasions when a few more years' running experience would have helped, Mick thought. Unlike the first two runners, Jim slowed slightly as he approached the checkpoint. "Phew, bit of weather up here today," he said in his distinctive Scottish accent. "Just a little," Bill responded. "You're doing well. Third place. Steve and Davie are a few minutes ahead."

Jim Henderson had continued, leaving the checkpoint with perhaps a hint of reluctance. He hadn't got far. A moment or two later he'd been back, pointing down the hill, shouting for help. "Quick, come quick," he'd said to Mick and Bill as he reached them a second time. "Davie's lying on the rocks." And then: "He's in a bad way." At that moment Jim had leaned over and been violently sick.

And then everything had changed. Mick and Bill had moved into mountain rescue mode. A quick discussion to agree a course of action, and then its implementation: Mick ran down to the Bad Step, the rucksack containing all the first aid in his hand, Bill stayed behind, managed to get through by phone to race control. At the same time, he thrust a warm fleece jacket and tracksuit bottoms at Jim Henderson who was by now shivering uncontrollably. Put those on, he'd commanded. No more running for you today. There's a bivvy bag down there in my rucksack too, get in it.

Mick had returned. The message was a grave one. "Still alive, but touch and go I think," he said. They both looked up into the mist, thinking the same thought: there was no way the air ambulance could come in in this weather. It would be a stretcher job.

"Call out the team. Better stop the runners here, we can't let them carry on and find Davie. Tell them on Bowfell and at Esk Hause shelter to do the same," Mick told Bill.

The mountain rescue team had rushed up from Langdale on the hikers' path to Red Tarn. They'd found Davie barely conscious and losing blood. The only hope was to get him off the hill and to a hospital. Quickly but with great care they strapped him on to the stretcher, hurried back down the hill, got him into the ambulance at the bottom. The vehicle accelerated away, blue light flashing.

Five minutes later, just passing through Chapel Stile village, the driver turned the blue light off. Rather more slowly, the ambulance picked its way through the country roads to Keswick and Carlisle. There was no longer the need to rush. At the hospital in Carlisle, the ambulance made for a small side door. Davie's body, still on the stretcher, was taken in to the mortuary.

What Nick hadn't gleaned at the Old Dungeon Ghyll bar after the race he'd learned first hand on the phone from the *Enquirer* office on the Monday morning. He'd made the necessary calls with considerable reluctance, but he'd made them nonetheless. He'd found out through a contact at the mountain rescue group the names of the marshals involved, and he'd managed to get through to Mick Patterson. He'd prepared a set of questions to ask, and Mick had responded, clearly not precisely pleased to have to tell the story and not vouchsafing any extra information, but not refusing to answer either. It was an extraordinary thing, this journalism business, Nick thought: you asked people things, and almost invariably they would respond. Even when really they'd have been better off putting the phone down on you.

And then Nick had contacted the race organiser. This was even more difficult. He could imagine only too well what it must be like to organise a race and finish at the end of the day with one of the participants dead. Nick decided not to let on that he'd been in the race himself, or that he ran for Coniston and Hawkshead. Better just to play the journalist. Hating himself, Nick asked the tabloid questions:

Shouldn't the race have been cancelled beforehand? Wasn't it obvious that the weather was much too bad? Had there been a risk assessment?

There had been a short silence and a sigh at the other end of the phone, and a tired answer about the risks inherent in any mountain activity. It was enough for the quote Nick was needing for the story. He didn't press the point, simply terminated the call politely and hung up. Then he attacked the keyboard with unusual savagery, bashing out the paragraphs, not stopping until the last sentence was in and the whole thing saved in the system.

And now Molly was standing at his back, telling him in as many words that he'd written crap. And he had. Hateful bloody job.

Molly took a long suck on her cigarette, exhaling with a sign of pleasure. She had picked up on Nick's mood, and decided not to push it. "I think perhaps we'll run with your piece as it stands. It's acceptable... and the spelling is immaculate. Anyway, time's pressing, and there's been a chip pan fire in a kitchen in Staveley. Get me 300 words on it, would you mind?" she said.

Nick swung round on his chair, and smiled apologetically. He knew what she was doing and was grateful for it. They faced each other. Molly chose her words carefully. "But, you know Nick, I'd like us to come back to the story again in a week or two's time. The Peters family are well-known hereabouts. Lots of people know his parents. And then there are all the people whose kids were at school with him. We need to cover this in a bit more depth. I'd like you when you've had a breather to cover it again. Get me the personal angles. Talk to the girlfriend – I assume there was a girlfriend? Talk to that other runner, the one who'd thought he'd won the race. See what the police are thinking – is there going to be an inquest, for example? Give my mate George there a ring, he'll help you out." She paused. "But take your time. This isn't the Sunday Times, you know, we're happy with our pace of life up here in Cumbria. Take as long as you need."

She gave him a half-smile and turned. The red polka dots on her top wobbled over her breasts and she, and the canary-yellow top, disappeared behind the door. She certainly knew her trade, Nick thought as with a grimace he wafted away the stale smoke. She could have been editing a national daily, if she'd wanted. Yet here she was, stuck in the provinces, happy with the *Enquirer*. Strange how some people didn't seem bothered by ambition. Strange what people wanted from life.

Chapter 3

"What I can't understand is why it was Davie. Davie of all people."

It was Thursday evening and they were in the Black Bull in Coniston. Thursday was the regular pack run night for Nick's club and, as usual, after the hard work on the hills most of the runners had gravitated to the bar. Drinking a pint or two probably undid most of the good effects of the training, but too bad. The sociable aspect of the running was one of things Nick most enjoyed.

Today, though, the mood was very downbeat. The club committee had considered cancelling, but in the end had decided to proceed with the usual Thursday night run. It was the right decision. Everyone was still very shaken by the events of the previous Saturday. Talking about it together was the best thing possible, and that was what was happening, in groups and huddles around the room.

"I mean, Davie was so fantastic at running downhill. Any one of the rest of us might have lost our footing and slipped on the rocks, but not Davie."

Nick nodded in agreement. He was sharing a drink in a quiet corner of the bar with Lindsay Maddens, and it was Lindsay who was doing the talking. "I just can't understand it at all," she concluded.

"Though the rocks had got really wet and slippery. A moment's carelessness, maybe?" Nick contributed.

He liked Lindsay, and he knew she liked him. They were friends, good friends... but just good friends. There had been a time, a year or so back, when their friendship could very easily have become something more. There'd been one particular night, Nick recalled, when Lindsay had been round at his house, and they'd had a meal and shared a bottle of wine together, and they'd both known that the evening looked likely to finish in Nick's double bed upstairs. And yet they'd both held back. It was as if they'd known at some level that, rather than making them closer, the sex might have had the opposite effect, complicating their friendship, perhaps even threatening it altogether. Instead, the evening had ended with smiles and a great big hug at Nick's front door.

And indeed, if anything, they had grown closer as a consequence. Lindsay had gone on subsequently to have a fling with someone from Carlisle, a quantity surveyor or something, and Nick had genuinely been pleased. Her divorce had been as messy as Nick's own business with Ana, but Lindsay was a good ten years younger than him, still young enough to have children and still looking for the man to have them with. Nick himself had stayed partner-less since that evening... though not entirely for want of trying.

This Thursday, however, his regular drink with Lindsay was proving slightly difficult for him. The problem was that he was now engaged professionally with the story of Davie's death. He already knew more than Lindsay, or indeed anyone else in the club, about some aspects of the affair but was for the time being unable to share what he knew.

"And another thing, nobody seems to know anything about the funeral. The longer it's delayed, the more this all seems unfinished business," Lindsay went on.

"Yes, well, there are various formalities which you have to go through when someone has an accident," Nick replied.

This was the best he could offer. The previous day, he'd had a lunchtime drink with Detective Inspector George Mulholland, Molly's number one contact with the local constabulary. George was Cumbrian to the core and delightfully old-school, not averse to a drink, and not averse either to a quiet natter with the press when the chance arose. He'd been at school with Molly, and Nick wondered whether there was still a little flame burning for her somewhere there. Or perhaps he just knew that information could flow both ways – Molly might sometimes be prepared to let slip something which could help him in his own job.

George opined to Nick over the glasses of Jennings' Cumberland ale that fell-running was plain bonkers, and that it was astonishing that the previous weekend's accident didn't happen all the time. The police weren't anticipating having to do much more than they had already done, which was basically just to let the coroner's office know.

"Will there be an inquest, do you think?" Nick had asked.

"Shouldn't think so, old boy. You've got to bring in the coroner when there's a sudden death like this, it's routine. But nine times out of ten that's the end of it. There's only about 20,000 inquests each year in the whole country. Basically, if there's a knife sticking out of someone's back or a note in their hip pocket saying they want to top themselves, well then it's pretty obvious that the old inquest machinery will have to start chugging away. Otherwise..."

The policeman gave a shrug and took a gulp of beer. "Still, the coroner's ordered a PM. Coroners tend to be keen on them. They probably all play golf with the pathologists," he went on.

"Post mortem."

"Exactly that. Bit of a messy affair, but fortunately families don't normally know what it entails. There'll be a toxicological report too, of course. Your runner chap wouldn't have done substances, would he? Maybe something to help him run that little bit better?"

"We're not talking about the Tour de France. Fell-runners are just a bunch of outdoor enthusiasts enjoying the mountains," Nick had replied.

"Just asking. Surprising what some people are prepared to do to their bodies. It's the compulsion to win which can drive them on. I had the case of that rugby league player over on the coast a few years back, for example." Mulholland went on to give details of some unpleasant little case which, he said, Molly would remember. Nick momentarily dipped out of the conversation. He had an image of a cold white room in Carlisle hospital where a man (yes, it would surely be a man) could at that very moment be picking up his scalpels and casually carving up the body of one of Britain's finest young athletes. Nick shuddered.

"So nothing really to help you with, I'm afraid. Of course, it might have been different if it had been old Pa Peters."

"Sorry?" Nick was back, paying attention.

"Molly not told you? We had a little bit of business with Peters' father a year or two back. He'd been doing a regular booze run across to Calais with his wagon. Got greedy, was going down sometimes twice a week, customs had to do something. I'm not telling you tales out of school, it's all there in the public domain. Got a whopping fine. Probably got off lightly, actually." George paused, finished his beer, and carried on talking.

"Anyway, what brings you up to our little backwater? Londoner, aren't you, I could tell from the accent. Problems down there in the Smoke?"

Nick had muttered something appropriately corny about heeding the call of the wild, and George Mulholland seemed satisfied. "But look after Molly Everett, won't you?" he went on. "Make sure she doesn't work herself too hard. Or make you work too hard either, for that matter. Get the work-life balance right, I always say. Actually, I've never been sure about the work bit of that, just give me the life."

Perhaps the beer had had its effect, but George Mulholland was becoming more and more avuncular as the afternoon went on. Though Nick wasn't entirely convinced. This man was a detective inspector, where it could sometimes be very useful to act dumber than you were. Nick smiled back politely and they'd left the pub to go their separate ways.

And now Nick was sipping another beer in another Cumbrian pub. Lindsay and he had been joined by a few others from the club, and the conversation had moved on. As if in reaction to the mood at the start of the evening, a certain black humour had crept in.

"Open and shut case, it was Steve Miller of course. Needed Davie out of the way for the Championship, hung around in the mist at the top of the Bad Step until Davie caught him up and then – oh, whoops, sorry, must have pushed you over the edge," one of the others said.

"Peter, that's in really bad taste," someone else replied.

"Anyway, have you heard? The English Championships is in complete confusion." This was Lindsay again. "Because Bowfell was cancelled, they don't know what to do about the gold medal. On the basis of the first five races, Davie has won. Or Jim Henderson if – er – if Davie is no longer eligible. But Steve's first place on Saturday would have given the Championship to him. They've talked about a replacement race but no-one wants that. Steve Miller's not too happy, and you can understand why."

"Though at least he's still alive. It brings it home to you, something like this." The speaker was the man called Peter. "We're the lucky ones. We've been out on the fells tonight, we're able to have a drink – and guess what, it's my round."

Nick smiled, but declined the offer. He had brought the car round to the pub, and had to make the drive home. But there was another reason. Peter's comments earlier, though meant as a joke, had worried Nick. He couldn't believe for a moment that a runner would murder another runner just to win a fell race – it was inconceivable. But at that moment he wanted time by himself to think about what could have gone wrong so fatally for Davie as he approached the Bad Step. More to the point, he also needed to find some time to transcribe what Davie's sister had said when he'd interviewed her earlier that day.

Chapter 4

Grief affects people in different ways. Some hide it away deep inside and seem able to carry on with some approximation of everyday life. For some, though, grief is paralysing and all-devouring.

Pauline had clearly been pole-axed by the death of her brother. It looked as if she hadn't slept since the weekend. Her eyes were bloodshot, her face taut with stress. She was, Nick knew from the research he'd already done, about two years older than Davie, which would make her in her late twenties. She looked to him as if she was forty.

He had door-stepped her. He had found her address in Kendal, and had driven across on Thursday morning. Her house was a small terrace in a quiet back street which looked as though it had been taken over by young professionals buying their first homes. Few of the houses had net curtains, so you could peer straight in: pine floors, bookshelves and Ikea sofas met Nick's glance. Pauline's own house was well-cared for, with shrubs in the small front garden. There was a For Sale sign from one of the local agencies beside the front gate. He opened the gate and approached the front door.

Door-stepping was one of those necessary journalistic techniques which didn't particularly get easier as you got older. For young reporters, it was something of a rite of passage. That first time you rang a front door, knowing that beyond the door was a middle-aged woman grieving for a husband killed in a work accident, or a girlfriend whose partner had ridden his motorbike into a tree, or a family whose young son had been accidentally drowned on a school expedition, was a moment of truth. Would you be able to deal with the situation? Would you be able to get what you had come there for, which – to be utterly candid – was the information you needed for the news story you were about to write? Because you were not a bereavement counsellor. You were there because, like it or not, the death was something your readers wanted to know about.

Nick had done his share of door-stepping when he'd first started out in journalism, before he'd got his break and moved to the Sunday Times. He felt out of practice, and he also felt nervous. But the secret was to get yourself invited in. Occasionally, you'd get the front door slammed straight back in your face, but not very often. Usually, people let you in. And once you were in, you'd cracked it.

He'd introduced himself to Pauline as being from the *Enquirer*, had made as if to walk in, and sure enough she had kept the door open and pointed him towards the kitchen table. But it hadn't initially been easy.

Nick had decided to start by asking about Davie's athletic career as a junior. It was, he thought, the best way to get Pauline to open up. He had been wrong.

"You must have been very proud of Davie's athletics prowess," he'd asked.

"I was," came a short reply.

"He was very talented, wasn't he?"

"Yes."

"Selected for England as a junior, that was quite an achievement."

"It was Britain," she corrected him.

And so the conversation had progressed, for what felt to Nick like an eternity. It was probably no more than five minutes. Finally Pauline had appeared to rouse herself. "I'd better offer you something to drink," she'd said. "Do you want tea or coffee? But it'll have to be black. The milk's gone off."

He opted for black tea, waited whilst Pauline filled two mugs with boiling water and dunked a teabag in each with a teaspoon. The resulting brew looked as black as water in a mountain tarn, but he drank it anyway.

"You were lucky to find me in," Pauline said, eventually. "Normally I'd be at work now. But they've given me compassionate leave this week."

She worked, he discovered with a little probing, for Cumbria Tourism. Her particular responsibility was to work with local hotels and guest houses who wanted to attract more walkers and cyclists. There was a specialist accreditation scheme available that allowed you to market yourself in walkers' handbooks or cyclists' magazines, if you made the grade. Pauline's role was to check whether each

23

establishment did make the grade. It involved looking at facilities like bike racks and drying rooms. She enjoyed the job, she said.

"God knows we need the tourists here. It's vital for our economy." She'd been at the University of Northumbria, done a Travel and Tourism Management degree, then moved back to the Lakes to put it into practice. She loved the fells, she said.

Nick sized her up. She had something of the same build as Davie, with a physique which looked like it too could be useful for fell racing. He asked her whether she had done much running. He was keen to get the conversation back to her brother.

"A little at school. And I would run on the fells with... with Davie," she said, finishing the sentence with some difficulty. "I play netball mostly, Goal attack is my position."

And then she abruptly fell silent. "I'm sorry, but I think you should go," she said.

Nick took a deep breath. "I know this is very difficult for you. I'm really sorry to have to ask you these questions. But, you know, Davie was well-known locally as a great mountain runner. I have to write something for the paper that adequately pays tribute to his life, and to what he achieved. I'm sure you understand. I want to ask you to tell me how he first discovered the fells."

Pauline sighed, settled again in her chair. Nick produced a small digital recorder, asked her permission, and set it on the table between them.

"It was during the school holidays mainly. The holidays were difficult for mum and dad. You see, dad's job meant that he was often away on the road, making a delivery somewhere down south, or even abroad sometimes. He's self-employed, so if he isn't driving he isn't making any money. And mum has always worked hard, too. So during the holidays they had to work out what to do with us."

Sometimes it had been Pauline's Nan, her mother's mother, who had taken the two children under her wing. She and her husband had farmed north of Crummock Water, and after his death she'd moved to a small bungalow near Rosthwaite. She still had a hill-farmer's fitness, though, and would drag Pauline and Davie up on to the fells at the back of her house. There were days spent exploring Grange Fell, more days on Maiden Moor and High Spy. Catbells was a particular favourite: high enough to be a mountain but small enough to be welcoming for children. Fantastic views of Derwentwater, too. "Catbells was great. Nan used to pretend that there were cats there, which we had to look out for. We never saw any, of course. Never heard any bells either," Pauline said.

Sometimes, other relatives would step in to help. Her dad's sister lived with her husband and their two children half-way down Eskdale, near where the Ravenglass and Eskdale railway terminates, Pauline said. Pauline's aunt also worked full time but Pauline's uncle worked shifts at Sellafield, which meant he could often arrange to take several days off during the week. His passion was industrial archaeology. He took the four children out exploring the remains of Cumbria's once significant mining industry. They rambled up Greenhead Gill from Grasmere to have a look at the remains of the Elizabethan lead mine there. They explored the old miners' bothy and the crushing mill at Hartsop Lead Mine, over beyond Kirkstone Pass. They spent endless summer days at Greenside, scrambling up to Keppel Cove Tarn where the water to drive the water turbines to drive the underground haulage at the mines was stored.

Most excitingly of all, when they were barely teenagers, they'd gone underground at Force Crag Mine, a couple of miles south of Braithwaite. Force Crag had been the last working mine in the Lake District, producing lead and zinc and other ores. They took silver from Force Crag too, Pauline said. If you knew what you were doing you could enter through one of the long Levels driven horizontally into the hillside, scramble down by means of ropes and half-rotten ladders left there by past explorers and eventually emerge into daylight after what seemed like hours by some spoil heaps at a completely different part of the hillside. "I expect they've stopped people doing it now. There were places where we looked down deep shafts into black nothingness, just beside where we were walking. My uncle probably shouldn't have taken us. He got a friend from work to come with us, but even so..."

Little by little, year by year, Pauline and Davie discovered their birthright, the mountains and fellsides of the Lake District. "Visitors here hardly know the area at all. Humans have worked these hills hard for the wealth within them," Pauline said. She paused. "Sorry, bit of an obsession with me. My degree dissertation was on industrial tourism. Though most people aren't interested. They just want a pretty view to point a camera at."

Pauline had relaxed. She seemed oblivious now to the little digital recorder on the table before her. Nick led the conversation gently on. He asked again about Davie's cross-country achievements, and this time Pauline was much more forthcoming. Her parents had done what they could to support him. She had too, she said. They'd been proud of his success. On one memorable occasion they'd travelled to Slovenia to be with him for the junior international competition. Nobody had offered to pay their fares, but her parents had cashed in some of their savings and turned it into a family holiday. And Davie had come in third, behind an Italian and a German but way ahead of all the other British juniors.

And then, later on? When Davie had turned twenty, for example, and could no longer count as a junior?

Pauline hesitated and once more seemed to be choosing her words with care. Well, Davie had left school at sixteen, she said, he hadn't wanted to follow her route into higher education. She'd encouraged him to think about going on to college, she'd even talked about the sports science degrees you could do these days at places like Loughborough. That would have been wonderful for him, she'd felt, a real chance to mingle with other top-class athletes from across all the different sports disciplines. But maybe she'd been too pushy. She sometimes acted too much the bossy older sister, she knew, and when she did Davie tended to react by doing the exact opposite of what she suggested. So anyway Davie had made his own life, and his own friends, and got himself a flat. And he had passed his class C large goods vehicle driving test. His dad had helped meet the cost, Nick gathered.

"Sometimes Davie and Dad went out together in Dad's wagon," Pauline said. She used the northern 'wagon', Nick noted. He himself would have said lorry. Ana had always said 'truck', the American way. What a rich resource the English language was. He forced himself back to what Pauline was saying.

"It meant that when Dad was up to his driving limit on the tachograph Davie could take over," she went on. "They went over to the continent a few times." Nick again momentarily stopped paying attention, pondering whether any of these could have been the booze trips to Calais mentioned by inspector Mulholland. "And sometimes Davie would drive the wagon just by himself, at weekends for example when Dad was resting. But really Davie begrudged the time he had to spend working. His love was his fell-running. That's what he turned to when he gave up the cross-country. He could be obsessive about things, you know."

She stopped. Nick asked the next question he had prepared.

"Yes, Davie was fantastically fit. He must have been pretty attractive to women. His girlfriend must be devastated."

Pauline looked up, suddenly cautious. "He doesn't have a girlfriend." Nick noted that she had slipped back into the present tense, as if Davie were still alive. "What makes you ask that?"

Nick retreated rapidly. "Sorry, an assumption. My mistake."

"I don't mean he was gay, he wasn't. I just mean that he didn't have a girlfriend," Pauline was back in the past tense, and had returned to the original abrupt manner with which she had greeted Nick.

"Of course. Listen, I won't intrude any more. I'm sorry to have caused you so much trouble." Nick played for time. "There's just one more thing I was going to ask you, though, a favour really. As you know, I'm writing a tribute to everything Davie achieved and I was wondering whether you could lend us a photo of him for us to use in the paper. I promise we'll take great care of it, and return it to you. Have you got something? – maybe that one over there?" Nick pointed to a snapshot propped up on the kitchen dresser, showing Davie in his Coniston and Hawkshead running vest and shorts, obviously just about to cross the finishing line of a local race.

Pauline handed it across to him. "Yes, I suppose so, OK. But please keep it safe." And then, abruptly, she seemed once more overcome by an overpowering grief. She dropped her head as she sat, holding it in her hands. The next words came out indistinctly, through sobs. "It was so awful to see his body with his running clothes all bloody," she muttered.

Nick spoke quietly. "I'm sure. I guess you had to go to the hospital, to identify him?" he asked.

Pauline didn't reply immediately, simply staring up at him. This was a woman who was still in shock, Nick thought. She needed help, not a local newspaper reporter pestering her with questions.

Eventually, she pulled herself together. "Yes, the hospital. Carlisle. Dad and Mum and I went. You've no idea what it was like."

And then: "I really wish you'd go away and leave me in peace."

He went. He snapped off the recorder, took the photo carefully, and made his own way to the front door, leaving Pauline still sitting in the kitchen chair, gaunt. The door closed behind him with a click. How terrible to lose a member of your family, he thought. How terrible to lose a brother, a younger brother.

He walked out of Pauline's small front garden, passing once again the For Sale sign. Damn, he'd meant to find out where she was moving, he realised. Oh well, too bad, you could never ask everything you wanted in an interview. The key was to get the important information. And, little by little he told himself, the feature he would shortly be writing was beginning to take shape. It might only be for the *Cumbrian Enquirer* but he was going to give it his best shot.

Chapter 5

The house which Nick had shared with Ana in north London had looked out on to a bare brick wall, the gable end of an old work unit in the street which came in at right angles to their own street. The street itself was something of a rat run between Kentish Town Road and neighbouring Camden Road. Like all parents of city children, they'd worried when their daughter Rosa was young about the speed of the traffic outside the front door. Parking of course was a nightmare, and for several years they'd simply decided not to bother with a car at all. Nick would get a hire car when they were off somewhere on a family trip. It was always Nick who drove. Ana's claim was that she still couldn't get used to driving on the wrong side of the road. Looking back now, Nick thought bitterly that it was a feeble excuse.

These days his view was different. His home looked out on the beautiful fells above the village of Grasmere.

More precisely, that was the view from the living room and the front bedroom. The back of the house had an equally wonderful view towards Helm Crag and the fells west of the village, dividing Grasmere from Great Langdale a little way over to the south and west. Nick had liked London and had considered himself an urban person, but really, who wouldn't rather live in the heart of the Cumbrian mountains than in a grubby London street of small overpriced terraced houses?

After the move, Nick had initially rented a nondescript flat in Ambleside whilst he'd looked around for a place to buy. To most British people, houses in sought-after Lakeland villages like Grasmere are unbelievably expensive. But Nick was moving north from London, and although Ana had demanded her half share of course, he had just about enough to make an offer. The place he'd eventually bought was on the northern edge of Grasmere village, away from the tourist cafés and gift shops. It was the middle of a small terrace made of the distinctive Cumbrian stone and slate construction, and was more of a small cottage than a house. But the kitchen and bathroom were relatively modern, and Nick was able to move straight in.

Shortly after the purchase, he'd realised with surprise that he was now living less than a mile away from the cottage where William Wordsworth had lived. Somehow he hadn't made the connection. As a writer, he was a little embarrassed to think that others might feel that he had chosen the village deliberately, that he was in some way wanting to compare himself with one of English literature's greatest. He comforted himself by recalling that Wordsworth had had more than a few off days himself. At his best Wordsworth was pure genius, but amongst the jewels of his writing he also managed to churn out a fair deal of mediocre stuff. Just like the rest of us in that respect, Nick thought.

Nick had turned the small second bedroom at the back into his office, keeping a sofa bed there for visitors. He'd hoped that Rosa would want to come regularly to visit him, but her life had changed too. She was now no longer the little girl he and Ana had taken to the swings in the children's playground round the corner in Kentish Town or for that matter the teenager, under age of course, who had worried her parents sick by going to clubs in the West End. Rosa had headed off to university just at the time when everything had fallen apart. One day the family had been celebrating the A level results she'd achieved and the confirmation of her place to read law at Warwick. Almost the next day, it seemed, Ana had told Nick across the breakfast table that it was all over. She had done her bit as a mother. She had seen Rosa grow up. Now she wanted something more from life. She was tired of London, she said. And she was tired of Nick, she added for good measure. Bye-bye.

Rosa told her father later that it had been obvious that this was coming, that anyone with any sensitivity would have realised that Ana was unhappy with her life and gearing up to go. Nick admitted ruefully that at some level he had known. He'd deliberately tried to block out the signs until it was too late.

They had met of course at the Independent, when Ana was working as the London correspondent for El País. The romance was a whirlwind one, passionate and all absorbing. Nick thought Ana the most beautiful woman imaginable. He wanted to spend every spare minute with her. What he really wanted, or at least what his body told

30

him continually that it wanted, was to have Ana in his arms, in bed. He wanted to touch her, run his hands through her long dark hair, play his lips over her delightfully red nipples, make love. His desire for sex was urgent and ever-present. Concentrating on work whilst working a few desks away from her in the office became almost too much to bear. Everything was focused on the day's end when they could leave their colleagues behind and be alone.

He'd first asked her out to a Spanish language film which was playing at the National Film Theatre on the South Bank. He'd done basic Spanish at school, and had worked out what to say. Pienso ir esta tarde al cine, para ver una película. Es en español. ¿Quizá quieres acompañarme? He'd wondered momentarily whether the 'tu' form might seem over familiar, but on the other hand he was inviting her out and the formal Usted form would have seemed utterly inappropriate. Ana had replied in English. "Are you asking me out for a date, Nick?" She called him Neek. Ana had always had a problem with the short English vowel sounds. "Because if so that would be very nice. Though let's speak English. Your Spanish is very good, but don't be offended if I tell you that it's not as good as my English." She'd laughed her great big captivating Ana laugh.

Later she would explain to Nick that his linguistic efforts weren't quite as appropriate as he'd hoped. She was from Sabadell, the old textile city twenty kilometres or so north-west of Barcelona. Though she wrote for El País every day in Spanish, her mother tongue at home had been Catalan, she said, a small gesture of defiance by her parents against Franco's proscription of the tongue. Later still she would teach Nick some Catalan, initially for those conversations all parents have when they don't particularly want their children understanding. Rosa, of course, rapidly made sure she could understand. She had become almost bilingual by the time she was ten, and could pass for local when she and her partner took trips to Barcelona.

The baby who was Rosa had arrived quickly, not quite to plan, only a year or so after the start of Nick and Ana's relationship. They loved this beautiful child that, together, they had brought into the world. But Rosa's arrival brought some difficult decisions. They both had their careers. Ana's stint at the London desk of El País was coming to an end, and her paper would expect her to move, perhaps to Madrid, to Barcelona, or to another posting abroad. Nick was thriving at the Indy. They struggled to work out the best way forward, and in the end Ana made the career sacrifice. She gave in her notice to El País and started doing freelance translating work for a range of companies and marketing concerns. It wasn't precisely rewarding work, but they'd seen it as a stop-gap. The plan was, after eighteen months or so, for Rosa to have a baby brother or sister. But despite the parents' best efforts, no second child materialised. Rosa was a *filla única*.

And then, eighteen years after Rosa's birth, Ana had decided that she wanted her career back. Her move from Kentish Town to an apartment in the slightly grotty area of Barcelona between Eixample and the harbour had been abrupt. She must have kept her old press contacts alive. She quickly found a job with La Vanguardia, Barcelona's venerable Spanish language newspaper, and then switched to El Periódico, the daily newspaper which manages the rare feat of coming out daily in two completely separate editions, Spanish and Catalan. And with these new jobs had come a new man. His name was Jordi. You said it with a soft 'j'.

Rosa had relayed this to her father, in abbreviated form. Nick and Ana had lived together without marrying but their separation was as spectacularly messy as the worst divorce. From almost that first morning, they had resorted to communicating with each other through solicitors. Nick hadn't even been given Ana's address in Barcelona. Almost the only tangible evidence remaining of those eighteen years of his life – leaving aside the daughter whom he loved dearly – were some old photos of the three of them together on holiday, a beginner's Catalan grammar book and a few CDs, the latter old birthday presents from Ana. The other thing remaining was the mountain-sized hole in his heart.

So life had changed. And, Nick thought to himself, he was, most of the time, more or less happy with his life. He'd tried looking for a new relationship, approaching the task in the spirit of journalistic endeavour, working his way in turn through the lonely hearts sections of each of the broadsheet newspapers. He'd begun with the Indy, then tried the Guardian's Soulmates, switched to the Times, and would soon be having to see if the FT could come up with anyone. Along the way there had been a English teacher from Lancaster, a video producer from Newcastle, an arts administrator from Stockport (long drive home), and a speech therapist from just down the road in Windermere. There had been some pleasant evenings, a little bit of sex, but nothing which had lasted. And then of course there was the close friendship that had developed with Lindsay. But he was used now to having the double bed in the front bedroom to himself, able to watch DVDs on the bedside TV until well after midnight if he wanted or to stretch out across the full width of the king-size duvet. And there was nobody to complain at breakfast that he had left his muddy running shoes at the bottom of the stairs.

Nick was, however, sorry not to see more of Rosa – she'd only been up to visit him three or four times in Grasmere (really, he thought, he could have saved himself the expense of buying that spare room sofa bed). Instead, they spoke on the phone frequently and he met up with her a few times a year in London, when he went down there on work. Curiously, Rosa was now herself living back in Kentish Town, or more precisely in a flat in nearby Tufnell Park. She'd graduated with a good 2.1, and had been taken on immediately by one of the big legal firms in the City. Her specialism was international commercial law, which Nick thought a dreary sort of business to be in but which his daughter obviously loved. The other passion in her life was her partner. They'd met in the very first week of university at Warwick and it was clearly love at first sight on both sides. Rosa and Becky had become an item almost immediately and had been inseparable ever since. After the initial surprise at Rosa's sexuality ("Oh dad, how could you not have known?" she'd rebuked him), Nick had grown to be almost as fond of Becky as he was of his own daughter. Though Becky had still not made it to the Lakes. It's an awful long way for a weekend had been her excuse.

So the sofa bed in Nick's office had developed a second life, as a key part of the filing system for his book. There was supposed to be a plan. Papers, press cuttings and reports on the technology of nuclear power were to be put at the left hand end of the sofa. The middle was for the material Nick has collected from opponents of the industry, including some useful stuff his main contact at Greenpeace had given him last time they'd met up in London. The pile on the right was intended for business information about the major global companies in the nuclear power industry, their annual reports, detailed analysts' reports, that kind of thing.

In reality, the system had broken down. The piles had become jumbled, and the papers had spread off the sofa on to the carpet beside Nick's desk. A rickety old card table had also been pressed into use, and this too was piled high with material. It was not the way Nick liked to work and he was annoyed with himself for being disorganised. However, he had to admit that the chaos around him rather reflected the way the book was currently shaping up.

And it was the book which he had to focus on now. He was at his desk, working through the day's crop of emails and, in between, glancing up to look at the fells beyond the window. It was Friday morning, and a nice day out there, rather too nice to waste indoors. Still... he took a slug of half-cold coffee from the mug beside him. One of his tasks today was to finalise the arrangements for a press facility trip he was trying to set up to the south of France. It sounded idyllic but unfortunately it was not to Nice or Cannes or the Luberon vineyards that he would be going. No, the plan was to get the PR people to take him round the industrial complex at Cadarache where the French state was investing vast sums in what could be the next generation of nuclear reactors. Cadarache was a sprawling mass of concrete surrounded by a perimeter fence. It was not in any tourist guide to Provence. Sometimes Nick thought he'd perhaps chosen the wrong theme for his book.

He had at least managed a short run before breakfast, pulling on the fell shoes and taking himself up on the footpath which runs up to Helm Crag. On the way back he'd called in to Barneys the newsagents and picked up his copy of that week's *Enquirer*. He'd read through it with a professional eye as he had munched some toast for breakfast. His piece about Davie Peters had failed to stay on the front page, he noticed, bumped off by a heart-warming tale of a mother from Cockermouth who had donated one of her kidneys to help save the life of her eight-year old son. Nick agreed with Molly's editorial judgement: that was definitely the right choice for the page one lead. A photo, showing the mother smiling alongside a cheeky-faced young lad, accompanied the piece.

Nick found his Peters story was now the page five lead. The headline Molly had come up with was almost as bland, he felt, as the way he'd written the news-piece itself: *Local runner dies in fell-race fall* was all it said. The story was illustrated with a rather fuzzy photo of Davie, which Nick suspected had been found somewhere in the picture library and was probably a year or two old. He would keep Pauline's photo to run next time round.

His mind stayed on the story, however, after he'd made his way upstairs to start the day's work. According to the work schedule he'd set himself when Molly had first offered him casual shifts, Mondays to Wednesdays were to be *Enquirer* days, Thursdays and Fridays were reserved for *Nuclear Power: Yes Please?*, whilst the weekend was supposed to be a strict no-work zone. In practice, he found it hard to keep to this pattern. This week, for example, he had already borrowed Thursday book-time to drive across to Kendal to get the interview with Pauline. Today, too, the work on the book would have to be curtailed. He'd allowed himself to fix an interview after lunch with Davie's old headmaster. Come round about 3 o'clock, the man had suggested when Nick had rung him up the previous day. My wife will have the kettle on ready for you, and we'll try to rustle up a few scones and butter as well.

Nick sighed to himself. He was in danger of getting too involved in this story. He was forgetting one of the first things you learned in journalism, which was to know when to stop. You weren't a historian, you weren't an academic, you could never hope to write the definitive article about anything. You were simply a journalist, offering up to your readers your best précis of what you had gleaned from the research and interviews you'd managed to do in a limited period of time, and then clearing your head of all that information so that you could move on immediately to the next story. Why didn't he seem to be able to follow this rule this time? Why had Davie's death affected him quite so deeply?

He made himself think about Cadarache, skim-reading a French newspaper article he'd downloaded from the web. Another big French government subvention had recently been made. He paused momentarily, trying to remember whether quinze milliards was French for 15 million or billion… well, whatever it was a large amount of money. The nuclear industry knew how to attract it at the moment.

He printed out the article, and added it to the nearest pile on the sofa. Outside the autumnal sun shone down on the mountains and lakes of England's largest national park. But Friday was a working day. Nick turned resolutely back to the keyboard.

Chapter 6

The scones were duly served up, on a fine bone-china plate. The tea came from a matching tea-pot, and was carefully poured into matching cups.

Mr Richardson lived with his wife in a suburban avenue just outside Keswick town centre, close to the path which visitors took to the Lake District's fourth highest mountain, Skiddaw. They had moved there about six years earlier, it transpired, when Mr Richardson had taken retirement.

His first name was Anthony, but somehow the old-fashioned headmasterly aura which still seemed to surround him suggested to Nick that it was probably better to stick to the 'Mr'. Nick had been greeted at the front door and shown into the lounge, a chintzy room which he suspected Mrs Richardson had furnished. He never found out her first name. "Ah, this is my wife," was all Mr Richardson had said by way of introduction as she came in with the tea-tray. He'd turned to her and added: "It's the chap from the *Enquirer*, you know."

Whilst the wife busied herself back in the kitchen, Mr Richardson drew up a large armchair so that he was facing Nick across the glass coffee table. "Right, ready when you are," he'd said.

Nick pulled out his shorthand notebook. The former headteacher was clearly raring to go. "A terrible loss. It is always a tragedy when a young person dies. Of course, er, David was a very popular pupil," he began. "Can I pass you the sugar?"

"It's ten years or more since he was one of my alumni, but you don't forget a personality like that," he continued. The words tumbled out: Great sense of humour... Always had a ready smile... Perhaps not our most gifted child, but a pleasure to teach... Could I tempt you to another scone?

Nick's pencil began to slow down. It was as though Mr Richardson had prepared for this visit by going to some password protected internet site which only head teachers or former heads could access, full of the things you had to say to the press when one of your pupils had suffered a terrible mishap. Platitudes-are-us.co.uk, Nick thought. He found his pencil tracing out a new shorthand shape: a small semi-circular shape joined to a long upwards diagonal stroke which in turn linked to a deep vertical line. It was the Teeline shapes for the three letters c-r-p. You generally didn't need to include vowels when writing Teeline, you guessed the word from the sense.

Mr Richardson stopped, and smiled at Nick. "I hope that's been useful," he said. The prepared speech was obviously over and Nick suddenly realised that the one thing which any teacher could genuinely have said about Davie Peters had gone unsaid. Nick prompted: "And then you must remember those school sports days?"

"Yes, of course, David was very good at sports," Mr Richardson responded.

"His athletics career. Having a pupil running for his county, and then for his country, that was quite something for your school I imagine."

"Oh, yes, you're quite right." But Mr Richardson seemed to have dried up. Nick closed the notebook with a snap, and stood up.

"Very kind of you to see me, Mr Richardson. I do appreciate it." And with what he hoped didn't appear indecent haste, Nick scuttled to the front door. He had just wasted a half hour of his life, he told himself.

He drove back through Keswick town centre, turning down the A591 and passing Thirlmere, the lake which gives Manchester its drinking water. On an impulse, he decided not to turn off home when he reached Grasmere but to carry on to Ambleside. He had known that Davie had lived in Ambleside, in a flat somewhere, and had looked up the address in the running club's membership list which everyone was given each year at sub renewal time. Without quite knowing why, Nick was curious to see the flat. With difficulty he found a parking place ten minutes away, and walked back.

Even on an October weekday there were plenty of tourists filling up the town. Not many of them, however, seemed to be visiting the few small shops in the street where Davie had lived. It was what estate agents would probably call a secondary shopping area, which was another way of saying that it wasn't really a shopping area at all. It was the sort of place where you might end up running a shop if you'd taken early retirement, had decided to put your lump sum into a little retail business in the Lakes, and didn't know any better. Nick suspected that shops lasted here on average for a couple of years before one owner retreated, defeated and broke, and another arrived with their pension lump sum at the ready.

As Nick has known, Davie's flat was above one of these shops. What he hadn't known was that it was a gift shop, with a stock dedicated entirely to merchandise related to sheep. It took Nick a moment or two to work the name out, and he wished he hadn't. The shop was called Baa Baa Baa, Baa Baa Baa Anne.

Who would imagine that one small shop could hold quite so much tat? Looking through the window Nick could see sheep rucksacks, sheep hot water bottles, sheep hats, sheep scarves. There were porcelain sheep with 'Ambleside' written on them, and big fluffy toy sheep with words across their bellies like I♥The Lakes. To one side was the greetings cards section of the shop, and Nick saw that each carried its own suitable message. I Love Ewe read one. Be my Ram-bo said another. For flock's sake give me a hug, read a third.

Both the shop and the upstairs flat shared a common front door. If you were a customer you turned left, to go through another glass door into the shop. The flat had its own second door, with a glass panel in it which showed a flight of stairs steeply ascending up to first floor level. The panel meant that Nick could look straight through on to the bottom step. From the pile of post which was there, it didn't look as if anyone from the family had been round in the six days since Davie had died. It didn't look either as if the post itself would be much fun to open. Almost all the envelopes were the sort which carried credit card statements or household bills. Nick wondered whether it would be Pauline or her parents who would have to wade through that lot.

"You one of those debt collectors, then?" The voice came from behind him, and made Nick jump. "Because if you are, you're too late now."

Nick turned round. The man from the sheep shop had being watching him, and had come across to the front door.

"Look at this."

The man had a newspaper in his hand, which after a moment Nick identified as the current issue of the *Enquirer*. After a further moment, he realised that he was being invited to read his own lead story on page 5.

"Gone and got himself killed." The man accompanied this remark with a bitter sort of laugh. His general demeanour, grumpiness personified, went rather incongruously with the air of jollity which the shop was obviously trying to cultivate. Customers must be in particularly short supply at the moment. Nick followed the man into the shop.

The shopkeeper had carried on talking, to himself as much as to Nick. "I should never have let him have the flat," he grumbled. "Ripped me off something rotten, he did. Any idea how much he owed me?" Nick realised that no reply was expected. The answer came: "Three months' rent. Three months! And here I am expected to pay all my bills on time, or get the bailiffs at the front door. You'd never guess how much the council duns me for their business rates. Or the heating bills."

Nick admitted that he couldn't guess. The man recommenced. "Just last week, he promised he'd pay up all the arrears. Said he'd got some money coming in. Said he'd give it to me Monday. Idiot that I was, I told him that would be OK. And now this. Fell on some rocks, it says here. Must have known I'd have done him in myself if someone hadn't got there ahead of me."

Nick took a snap decision. "Yes, he owed us quite a bit too," he said. He wasn't quite sure why, but he decided that there might be some value in playing along with the debt collector persona he had been given. "But our solicitors are sure we'll get it back from the estate. I'll see what I can do for you as well, if you like. Give me a ring if you hear anyone moving about upstairs and I'll pop back. Here's my mobile number."

Nick scribbled the numbers down on a scrap of paper. This was not an occasion for his *Cumbrian Enquirer* business card, he thought. Then he looked around the shop. Clearly there was some sort of obligation to make a purchase before he could get himself back out into the street. His gaze fell on a bag of chocolate raisins, packaged up with a label which read Genuine Lake District Sheep Droppings. "Ah good, just what I need for a present," Nick lied, handing over a five pound note. The shopkeeper rummaged in the till to find the change. There was clearly very little money there. It was an easy prediction to make: the business was heading for bankruptcy. Or perhaps in its case baa-nkruptcy.

Walking back to the car, Nick had to admit to himself that Mr Sheep Shop had suggested a rather different take on Davie's life than that which Mr Richardson had proffered. He felt slightly sullied by what he had accidentally discovered. So Davie had had money problems: lots of people did, it was a feature of the economic crisis that everyone had been living through. It hadn't stopped Davie from being able to run across the Cumbrian mountain tops like a god. That was what Nick's feature would have to celebrate: the heights of achievement which humans can reach, not the humdrum problems of daily life that drag them down.

His mobile rang, just as he had reached his car and was getting out the ignition key.

"Hope I'm not disturbing you, old boy. Wouldn't want to interrupt a journalist in his quest for a scoop." The caller hadn't introduced himself, but Nick recognised the voice immediately.

"Ah, detective inspector. Good to hear from you."

"I was wondering whether you had stopped work yet for the weekend. Or is Molly still keeping your nose to the grindstone? By the way, call me George."

"No grindstones in sight at the moment, George. I'm actually in Ambleside, just about to head home to crack open a beer."

"Ah, well there I have the advantage on you. I'm sitting in the Woolpack in Eskdale with a Lakeland Stunner."

"That sounds very pleasant. Do I take it you're referring to a person or to a beer? Or perhaps both?"

"Just the beer, sadly. My better half is very tolerant of my foibles, but not quite that tolerant."

"Well, George, I'm tempted to drive across to join you, but by the time I've driven all the way over into Eskdale I rather suspect that your Lakeland Stunner may be no more. And I wouldn't want your wife to have to complain that I had kept you away from your dinner. "

"I fear you may be right. A second Lakeland Stunner could be too much for me for one evening, even with your own pleasant companionship. Omne nimium vertitur in vitium."

"Sorry?"

"Every excess becomes a vice."

"Indeed, I'm sure it does. Er – was there a reason for you to ring me?"

"Forgive me, old boy. You're allowing an elderly man to ramble on. Just thought you might be interested to know about the PM."

"Prime minister."

"Post mortem."

"Of course. You mean Davie Peters, I assume?"

"Yes, young Peters. Poor lad. Anyway, looks like the coroner is going to call for further tests. I don't think it's anything untoward. The word is that they think it was most likely an accident. Still, there's some bruising on the face and torso which the pathologist couldn't quite explain. So they've asked us to keep the file open just a little bit longer."

"More work for you, by the sound of it, George."

"Not really. The boys and girls in the uniformed branch will take a couple of statements from some of the race organiser people, nothing much more than that I'd think."

"Well, anyway, it's kind of you to let me know."

"Not at all. Now, one more thing, and this is rather important. Molly lent me a rather nice illustrated book of photographs of Windermere a few weeks back, and I want you to tell her that it's safe and sound and I have it ready to give back to her next time I'm anywhere near the office. Will you make sure she gets the message?"

"I will indeed, George. I'm sure Molly can spare the book a little longer. And, er, have a pleasant weekend."

"I certainly intend to, old boy. Bye for now."

The phone went dead. Nick started the car, extricated it from the parking place he was in, and headed for home. He was looking forward to that Friday evening drink more than ever.

Chapter 7

Saturday dawned bright. It was going to be a very pleasant Autumn weekend.

Across the national park, the Lake District tourist industry shook itself awake and prepared for a new day. Lights went on in kitchens.

Tourists come to the Lakes for a range of reasons. Some will be planning to spend the day pounding the summit of Skiddaw, some will be pounding the streets of Bowness looking for bargains in the shops. All, however, want to feel that they are getting their money's worth, and if there's a cooked English breakfast on offer in the hotel or B&B where they're staying then the chances are that they'll order it. Even if breakfast at home is normally a cup of coffee and a slice of toast.

There are around 800 businesses in the Lake District national park offering accommodation, and between them they provide well over 15,000 beds. Even if not all the beds are occupied all the time that still means a lot of people coming down the stairs every morning looking forward to fried egg, sausages, baked beans and bacon. Cumbria Tourism collates a great deal of information on the tourist sector in their patch, but not even they can tell you how many pigs give up their lives each year to provide the catering packs needed for all the cooked breakfasts.

Cumbria Tourism does know all about employment, however. This is geographically a very peripheral part of the country and there are areas of Cumbria, particularly out on the coast beyond the Lake District in the old mining areas near Whitehaven and Workington, which are some of the most economically depressed parts of England. So jobs are vital. Whilst there may be plenty of sheep on the fells, there are few jobs in farming any more. The nuclear complex at Sellafield helps the local economy but only to a limited extent. So when it comes to employment, the county of Cumbria is effectively dependent on the tourists coming and bringing their spending money with them.

Add up the jobs in the Lake District national park which tourism creates and you'll come up with a figure of around 11,000 full-time jobs. Though it's more complicated than this. Tourism is an industry which is notorious for its use of part-time, casual and seasonal workers, so that if you want to find out how many *people* get their living from tourism you'll have to do further sums.

Pauline Peters at Cumbria Tourism would be one of the people you'd be counting. Her mother Margaret would be another.

Margaret Peters' alarm was set for 6am during the week. Saturdays, however, were the busiest day and that meant each Friday night adjusting the little alarm clock hand so that it pointed at 5.30am. She needed time not just to get herself up and dressed, but also to get out to the country hotel on the road towards Coniston where she had been working for the past two years. Although she and her husband Gary ran a VW Polo as well as Gary's second-hand 18 ton DAF truck, most of the time she chose to cycle the six miles or so on an old upright bike. She quite liked the exercise, but she liked saving the cost of the petrol even more.

Her shift started at 7.15am and ran on until 2pm. The hotel technically offered breakfast from 6.30 in the morning, but in practice very few visitors at weekends ventured down that early to the glass conservatory at the back of the old Victorian building where breakfast was served. Until she arrived, Mick the chef or Patsy the kitchen assistant would cope. But thereafter serving the breakfast was her responsibility alone and sometimes it could get busy. The hotel had 28 bedrooms, 24 of them doubles, and it was sod's law that half the guests would all decide to arrive downstairs at the same time.

The hotel was by no means at the top end of the Lake District league table when it came to price, but nevertheless the standard charge for a double room came in at £140 per night. £70 per person, that was a hell of a lot of money. Margaret wondered how it was that people could still afford to have holidays at all in Britain these days. When Pauline and Davie had been kids, the whole family had been able to have a package in Spain for under £500.

But for your money you did get a bit of choice at breakfast. The full English cooked included Cumberland sausages and black pudding made by an organic farmer over in east Cumbria, in the Eden valley. Or you could order scrambled eggs (Cumbrian, free range) with smoked salmon. Or kippers. The kippers were from Scotland somewhere, as far as Margaret knew, and they smelled out the kitchen something rotten. Still, some people ordered them.

She did breakfasts until 9.30am, or as soon thereafter as the last of the guests had gone. Then she changed aprons and began work on cleaning the bedrooms. This was hard work, but it was work she was well accustomed to.

The hotel management stipulated that ten minutes were allowed per bedroom. It was very tight, particularly if the hotel was close to full capacity, although she made it a matter of pride that she would complete the cleaning on schedule. New guests had access to their rooms after 2 anyway, so there was very little slack available.

You just needed to establish a routine. Margaret began each room by stripping the beds of their sheets and duvet covers and collecting up the used towels, dumping them in the canvas sack out on the landing which would later go off to one of the commercial laundries serving the Cumbrian hotel industry. Next she would focus on the bathroom, carefully cleaning the bath and hand basin and wiping down the mirror. The toilet had its own cleaning materials and often needed a very good going over and the bathroom floor also needed to be swabbed down. Then it was time to go back to the main bedroom, putting the clean sheets on the bed and vacuuming the carpet thoroughly.

And then, as soon as one bedroom was finished, it was time to move on to the next. One down, twenty-seven to do.

Miles the manager had tried to be kind. He'd rung earlier in the week as soon as he'd heard about Davie, and had told her that she could take some of her holiday entitlement if she wanted. He'd get someone to cover for her, he said. But in the end, she'd chosen to come in to work. Monday, her usual day off in any case, she'd spent in tears, at home. A whole week like that and she would be suicidal, she thought. It didn't help that Gary had had a busy schedule of deliveries, which he absolutely had to meet and which had meant that he had been away overnight for a couple of days during the week. This was a time when she knew she needed other people around, to help her through.

And everyone at the hotel had done their best. Nevertheless there had been an embarrassment in the way they had related to her which she found hard to cope with. They wanted to show their sympathy, no doubt, but they didn't really know what to say. Some people even seemed to be deliberately avoiding being alone with her. Only the Polish lass Khrystyna on reception had really got it right. She'd been completely unaware of what had happened until late in the week, when someone else had shown her the article in the *Enquirer*. Then she'd rushed up to Margaret, put her arms around her and given her an enormous hug. "I am so sorry," she'd said, in her heavily accented English. "Really, I am so very sorry."

It had been awful when the policeman had come knocking. Saturday night it had been, about eight o'clock. Gary had gone for a drink in one of Ambleside's town centre pubs with some of his mates, and she was watching the X Factor on the television. When she'd first seen the police helmet, she'd thought that Davie had got himself into trouble. She was worried about what exactly he got up to on Sundays when Gary let him borrow the wagon. Well, Davie had got himself in trouble, of course, terribly so, but not in the way that she'd thought. It took her a few moments to understand what the policeman was trying to tell her. Very young the policeman was, probably the same age as Davie. Generally she and Gary tried to have as little to do with the police as possible, but this man you felt was doing his best to be kind. Not like the detective inspector character they'd had round to their house that time previously, who had seemed amiable enough, almost bumbling, but who had all the time been prising out the information he needed to stitch Gary up good and proper. She and Gary still hadn't really fully paid off the debts they'd had to take on to pay the fine.

The young policeman's visit had been the start of the nightmare. There had been the trip they'd had to take to Carlisle, 'to identify the body' those were the words someone had used to her. Awful, awful. Pauline who had come too had behaved really strangely, silent and withdrawn. Presumably it must have been the shock of the news, but Margaret had almost wished she and Gary had gone alone. Someone had shown them into the morgue all very matter-of-fact. Davie had been lying there lifeless, in some kind of hospital shroud.

Somehow she thought there would be people whose job it would be to help them get through an event like this. But it didn't seem as if there were. Instead, she'd found herself having to cope with an alien bureaucracy which wasn't designed to take her feelings into account. It had been a shock to discover that the body had to remain in the mortuary, and that they couldn't claim Davie immediately and start organising the funeral. And then they hadn't even been told that there was going to be a post mortem. Although apparently they had no right to stop it going ahead anyway.

The person who seemed to be pulling all the strings was the coroner. Margaret had been given his office number, but every time she rang it was the coroner's clerk, a woman called Nicola, who she got through to. Nicola seemed as if she was trying to help, but Margaret felt that actually her role was to fob off the relatives. Apparently the coroner's job wasn't to answer the phone himself.

At Nicola's suggestion they had got hold of an undertaker who had discussed what sort of ceremony they would want as soon as the coroner gave the OK for the body to be released. And Margaret's family and neighbours had rallied round and given her strength too. But still. She switched off the vacuum, did the final checks, and closed the door on bedroom 25. 26 and 27 had been empty the previous night, so that just left one single bedroom to complete. She would be away a few minutes after two. Gary was at home, and as soon as she got back she'd organise a light dinner for them both.

Across the other side of Windermere, Lindsay Maddens was also spending her Saturday working, also doing her bit for the tourist industry. She worked in the wholefood café in the village of Staveley which was something of an institution among outdoor enthusiasts. Cyclists made the detour into the village when they were in the southern Lakes and climbers and mountain walkers called in on their way home after a day on the hills. You could get a decent pasta bake, or a selection of salads, or if you preferred a proper bacon butty, all washed down with a strong cafetière of coffee. Lindsay worked primarily in the kitchen, but sometimes did the counter. There was a good atmosphere about the place, and a strong likelihood that some of her clubmates from Coniston and Hawkshead would call in at some point during the day.

She had taken the Saturday job in Staveley a year or so back, mainly because she was finding herself increasingly short of money. Really she was a planner by profession, and three days a week she worked in the planning department of the local council in Kendal. The problem was that the job was part of a job-share, and despite her best efforts she had failed to find a full-time job in any of the nearby councils. The only alternative would have been to have moved to another area of the country, and that was definitely not something she wanted to do. She'd lived in the Lake District all her adult life, and this was her home now.

She had discovered the area when she had been a student just down the road at Lancaster. Choosing Lancaster had been an inspired decision.

She was originally from Milton Keynes, the new town plonked down in the fields of north Buckinghamshire, so it was fantastic to be so close to real mountains. She joined the student hiking club and the fell-running club as well, and every weekend (and some weekdays too, when she should really have been at lectures) she and her friends piled into a minibus and made the short hop north on the M6 to the Lake District.

Choosing Greg had been a less inspired decision. It was classic, really. She'd started the relationship with him on the rebound, just after she'd split up from an old boyfriend of hers, Peter. They'd married almost immediately. It was a few years after she'd graduated. Greg was a couple of years older than her, and already getting established in his career. He worked for one of the multinational accountancy practices, as one of their many young and thrusting consultants called in by local councils dazzled by the idea that they were buying international expertise. Lindsay had been dazzled too. Together she and Greg had bought a house in Kendal, though Greg's work took him all over the country so that Lindsay found married life much lonelier than she expected. When she turned thirty, her thoughts turned increasingly to children, but Greg was passively resistant to the idea. More than ever he was focused on his career, and making money.

Just after their seventh wedding anniversary (Greg had been in London for the day itself), she discovered he had been having affairs. They parted, in a very acrimonious divorce. In her mid-thirties, Lindsay found herself single again.

Life since then hadn't always been easy, but it was a big improvement on married life in a suburban street in Kendal. She'd made some real friends in the running club which was now the focal point of her social life, people like Nick Potterton for example who'd just come through a very similar separation to her own. She and Nick had a lot in common, it was just a pity that he was more than ten years older than her.

Her shift at the café started at ten and lasted until five-thirty, when the day's trade was petering out. Working Saturdays did mean that she wasn't available to join other members of her club for Saturday fell races or training runs, though as it turned out she was quite relieved not to have been out on the hills for the Bowfell race the previous weekend. Anyway, Saturday evenings were all hers, as were Sundays.

Nick had phoned earlier, asking her what she was up to after work. He'd sounded a little needy, but Lindsay had had to tell him that she had already arranged a girls' night out with four or five of the other women from the club. Nights like these were organised every few weeks, and Lindsay enjoyed them enormously. There would be specific fell-runner conversation, of the kind that would be incomprehensible to anyone outside the sport and which generally consisted of discussions of past races (who had run well, who had run badly), future races (where the climbs were, how to choose the best line for a particular descent), and – a topic which could be relied on to provide endless scope for conversation – the latest varieties of fell-running shoes on the market. But there would also be the usual sort of gossip which any group of friends indulge in when they meet together. Lindsay knew that she'd be asked for all the low-down on how things were going with Phil.

The answer would be that they were going fine. In fact, she'd arranged to go up to Carlisle for the Sunday to be with him. Phil wasn't necessarily the sort of person she'd imagined having a relationship with, but he had an old-fashioned sort of sensitivity that she found quite endearing. He was sweet. He would do things like buy her red roses, or take her out for surprise fancy dinners. He was a chartered surveyor, which went quite well with Lindsay's planning background, but more to the point he was a keen road cyclist. Lindsay had recently started training for her first triathlon and was working hard on improving her cycling. They went out together on their bikes on the quiet roads north of Carlisle up towards the Solway Firth.

So Lindsay had had to turn down Nick's other suggestion, which was to go running somewhere on Sunday afternoon. She heard the note of disappointment in his voice which he tried to hide.

"By the way, I saw your article about Davie in the paper. I thought it was very good," she said, as some sort of response.

"Did you? Thank you," Nick replied. And then, after a pause: "By the way, you don't know whether he had a girlfriend, do you?"

"A girlfriend? Not sure. I'll ask the girls tonight if you like, one of them is bound to know."

"OK, thanks. Have a great time tonight. Tomorrow, too, of course. Probably see you Thursday at the pack run?"

"I should be there. See you then, Nick."

Lindsay pushed the little red button on her mobile. In Grasmere, Nick put down the receiver on his landline phone.

Chapter 8

As it turned out, Nick had also spent Saturday working. The disruptions of the week had meant that he had done much less on the book than he had anticipated, so he decided to sacrifice one of the days of the weekend to catch up.

The pitch he'd successfully made to the publisher was this: nuclear power was a technology and an industry which had seemed twenty-five years earlier to be gone for good. Chernobyl in 1986 had been the last and the most catastrophic of a number of major accidents worldwide which had left the industry reeling and the politicians swearing that they would never again authorise another nuclear plant to be constructed. Yet at the start of the twenty-first century, the industry had risen like a phoenix. Suddenly new nuclear plants had been commissioned, and a lot of money was being made. Nick's book would tell the story of this secretive industry which, even after the Japanese tsunami hit Fukushima, some people still insisted was a safe way of producing power.

His opening chapter was already completed, and he was fairly pleased with how it had shaped up. He had decided to begin on October 10th 1957, the day when the graphite core of the nuclear reactor at Windscale – the Cumbrian site which afterwards changed its name to Sellafield – caught fire. Eleven tons of uranium blazed away before the fire was eventually extinguished. Some said that, if things had just gone a little differently, this was the day when we could have lost the north-west of England for good, and maybe parts of Wales and Ireland as well. In the event, the government bought up all the milk from the nearby countryside for a month, diluted it and dumped it at sea. The official report of the incident was kept secret for thirty years.

Nick told the Windscale story briefly, trying to explain to his readers how the first generation of nuclear reactors, like ill-fated Windscale Pile No 1 where the accident occurred, were the result of the need during the cold war to produce plutonium for nuclear weapons systems. His narrative then went forward to the big expansion of civil nuclear power in the 1960s and to the anti-nuclear movement which began to build up in the 1970s, when the smiley sun logo with its slogan *Nuclear Power, No Thanks* could be seen (suitably translated into all sorts of major and obscure languages) at demonstrations around the world. The story then pitched up in 1979 in Pennsylvania, at Three Mile Island, where a serious accident in a pressurised nuclear generator had caused the reactor core to go partially into meltdown. Rather unhelpfully for the nuclear industry, the accident happened less than a fortnight after Hollywood had released the China Syndrome, a fictional account of a very similar disaster. And then, a few more years on, came Chernobyl in the Ukraine.

Nick had decided that an appropriate way to finish the first chapter would be to bring the reader back to the Lake District. The weather immediately after the Chernobyl disaster had been unkind to much of northern Europe, with winds taking the clouds from the direction of Chernobyl north and west. The rain which fell over high ground, including the mountains of Cumbria, was seriously contaminated with radioactivity and the radioactive particles passed easily from the peaty soil to the grass, and then in turn to the sheep which grazed on the grass. More than two and a half decades later, a handful of Lake District farms were still being monitored regularly by the Food Standards Agency with the sheep there deemed to be too contaminated to be released into the food chain. Nick had interviewed some of the farmers affected, hearing their tales of the frustration of spending years of their lives farming livestock for no purpose at all other than to be able to claim the compensation. It was the personal details like this, Nick hoped, which would make what might otherwise be a worthy but specialist book accessible to the general public. It was after all, he told himself, what good journalism was supposed to be all about.

He stopped working at around four, and began to think about the rest of the weekend. He'd phoned Lindsay earlier to see what she was doing and had also rung around to a few other friends in the running club, but everyone seemed to be committed. These were the times when it wasn't always easy to be single. Still, the forecast for the Sunday was quite good (what a change from the previous weekend) and the hills were calling. Nick picked up the calendar of fell races which the Fellrunners' Association produced each year and skimmed through. There was a short morning race being organised in the Yorkshire Dales from the village of Austwick up to the top of Ingleborough and back, he noticed. It would be a low-key affair with perhaps only a hundred or so runners, and at only four miles he'd be back down at the finish in well under the hour. Austwick wasn't much more than an hour away down the A65.

A pleasant little race like that could help exorcise the memories of the previous Saturday, he thought. Could stop him obsessing quite so much about the Davie Peters story.

At which point he immediately thought again about his article, and had a brainwave. When she'd asked him to follow up his original newspiece for the *Enquirer*, Molly had suggested vaguely to Nick that he talk to Davie's girlfriend. Well, he'd tried to track such a girlfriend down but at the moment the trail was cold. But Molly had also muttered something about talking to the runner who had come in first at Bowfell. Steve Miller. Nick had rather dismissed the idea from his head – Steve lived across in the Leeds area, too far away to make a special journey.

But the Austwick fell race was, relatively speaking, on Steve's doorstep. Just supposing? Nick decided that when he got his running kit ready for the race he'd also put his digital recorder in the sports bag.

There were fewer runners than Nick had expected at the start line, but Nick spotted the mop of black hair he was looking for ahead of him at the start line. He went across to introduce himself. And when it was all over, after the lung-busting climb up to the Iron Age hill fort at the summit of Ingleborough and the screamingly fast descent back down to Austwick, after the prize-giving too, Nick, Steve and Steve's partner Pennie sat down together at one of the tables in the garden of the Game Cock, Austwick's village pub.

Nick's blue and green running vest, now somewhat muddy from the race, had been a good enough introduction for Steve; fell-runners were a small community, fell-runners were family. Nick had been scrupulous in explaining his role for the *Enquirer*: Steve said he'd be delighted to help.

The garden table held the drinks Nick had bought at the bar on the table, but it also carried the spoils from the prize-giving. Steve had, predictably, come in first. In front of him was the bottle of red wine he'd been given as well as a white envelope which Nick suspected enclosed a gift voucher from a nearby running shop. Pennie too had a bottle of wine in front of her. She'd had a good run, just beating another woman runner at the finish funnel to come in as the third female. Nick had a bottle of wine beside him as well.

"Congratulations Steve, great run. You too, Pennie," Nick said.

"Well done on your prize too," Steve responded. They all laughed. Nick had run well, but nowhere near enough to be amongst the prizewinners. The wine had come his way as one of the four spot prizes randomly awarded by the race organiser to runners further back in the field. It was a feature of some fell races, recognition that everyone who took part contributed to the success of a race. Nick had won a couple of spot prizes previously in his running career. It was always a welcome surprise when it happened.

The ice had been broken. The digital recorder was placed on an upturned ashtray, and they began to talk about Bowfell. Firstly, about the weather.

"The clag was well and truly down. I was pleased not to go wrong at Esk Pike," Steve said.

"I took a terrible line around Rossett Pike. I had a feeling that I was going to miss Angle Tarn altogether and find myself heading straight down towards Borrowdale," Nick replied.

"You wouldn't have been the first to go spectacularly wrong. My worst ever mistake was ending up on Dow Crag rather than the Old Man during the Coniston race. Mind you, the weather was even worse that day. Pretty well the whole field followed me, which was a touch embarrassing."

Steve Miller was engaging, easy to talk to. You could tell he was a good teacher. He looked you in the eyes, slightly unnervingly, for his own eyes were an almost unnatural blue colour. You felt drawn in, Nick felt, unable to break the gaze. Obliged to trust him and what he was saying.

The conversation, inevitably, turned to Davie Peters' death. Steve said that it was risk they all took in engaging with the mountains.

"I've had to deal with a couple of fatalities with our mountain rescue team," he said. "It always shakes you up more than you expect. I guess I was lucky not to be the person who came across Davie at the Bad Step."

"Were you friends?" Nick asked.

"Well, we knew each other, but, no, I wouldn't say we were friends. I only saw him at races of course, and at races he was the competition!"

Steve took a sip from the beer glass in front of him.

"If I'm honest, I'd have to say that I didn't really like him," he went on. "There was something about his character I never really understood. Still, what a phenomenal athlete.

"And keen to win every race he ran," Steve went on. "You know, he bet me £100 back at Edale in March that he'd walk off with the English Championships gold medal this year. I told him that he was wrong, that I was going to win, but that he obviously didn't how much teachers got paid if he thought I could afford wagers like that. We agreed to make it a fiver each."

"Tell me how you got down the Bad Step," Nick asked.

"The Bad Step? Well, I was relieved to be first to it, because I knew Davie was going to have the edge on me on the descent. There was almost no visibility up there, of course. I barely saw the marshals on Long Top, they loomed up out of the cloud as I approached. I got down the Bad Step no problem, and picked up the trod that takes you almost all the way to Red Tarn."

"Davie must have lost his footing?"

"Well, I suppose so, although it wasn't like him. Mind you, the weather was so bad that anything could have happened up there that day. You could have hidden a regiment of the British army behind the rocks and nobody would ever have known they'd been there."

Steve stopped and appeared to be thinking.

"Actually, it's curious, I haven't mentioned this before, but I had a strange feeling just before the Bad Step that there *was* somebody else up there. Sort of trying to avoid being too obvious. You know how you get a sixth sense when the clag's down and you can't really use your eyes. Somebody seemed to emerge towards me as I came off Long Top, and then withdraw again. But maybe it was just a walker. Or it could have been an animal, a fox or something." He paused again. "Maybe I'm imagining things. After something like an accident happens, I think your memory actually becomes really unreliable."

The conversation moved on, and Nick asked about the English Championship. "Well, I was all wound up to win it at Bowfell, but really it all fades into insignificance now." Nick looked up, suddenly sensing that Steve had stopped being entirely convincing. Everyone knew how much he had coveted that prize.

"Anyway I've got next year to look forward to," Steve went on. "Unlike Davie, I'm afraid."

"He lost his bet."

"He lost his life," Steve replied.

A light breeze had got up and the sky had clouded. Nick had pulled a long-sleeved top over his vest, but was beginning to feel he needed to get some warmer clothes on. Pennie, too, by the look of it felt the same way. Together, the three of them finished their drinks and got up to head back to the race car park.

"Good to talk, Nick. Hope the article goes well," Steve said. And then almost as an afterthought: "You know, someone else wants to talk to me about the Bowfell race. A detective rang a couple of days ago, and said he needed a statement off me. Just routine, he said. Detective inspector Mulligan from the Cumbrian police, I think that was the name."

"Mulholland, probably," Nick said. "I know him a little through work."

"Well, I told him where I lived and he said he'd drive across to meet me after school on Tuesday. I reckon that's about a five hour round trip. It seems to me that there can't be enough work for him if he has time to do that. Don't you have any crime in Cumbria?"

"Perhaps he wants a day out in the Dales on the way down?" Nick hazarded.

"Well, anyway, I said I'd help him as much as I could. Which frankly is hardly at all, I think."

"He'll be going through a box-ticking exercise," Nick replied, as they went their separate ways. But what he actually thought was that Mulholland had been telling him porkies. Hadn't he told Nick, or certainly implied, that he wasn't going to concern himself at all with the Davie Peters case? Yet here he was prepared to drive half way across northern England to take a statement from Steve.

Nick drove meditatively back up the A65, crossing over the M6 and taking the dual carriageway back to Windermere. His route home took him through Ambleside, and to his own surprise he found himself looking for a parking place. He was lucky: there was a place just a few yards from Baa, Baa, Baa.

The door up to Davie's flat had a bell beside it, and without quite knowing why Nick pushed the button. A bell rang upstairs, but nobody came down. Still, Nick noticed, there had been somebody there since his last visit. The pile of post he'd seen before had gone.

At that moment, he saw himself being watched from behind the shop till. "Oh it's you again," the man said as he entered once more the shop.

"Somebody been visiting?" Nick asked, gesturing with his thumb upstairs.

"There was a woman in the flat yesterday." The shopkeeper paused. "Sorry I didn't ring to let you know, I lost that bit of paper you gave me." He looked a little, well, sheepish.

Nick scribbled his number down a second time, as the man continued his account. Obviously, from the description, it had been Pauline who had been the visitor.

"She stayed about an hour. I told her as she left that I was owed my rent."

"And?" Nick prompted.

"She didn't say anything, just grimaced and walked out. Nobody cares about small shopkeepers these days."

"It must be difficult," Nick said, with what he hoped was a note of finality. He really didn't want a one-way conversation on hard times in small town retailing. "By the way, I don't think I know your name." He held out his hand.

The shopkeeper took the proffered hand. "Shepherd. John Shepherd. No, don't say anything, I've heard it all before."

I'm sure you have, thought Nick to himself as he walked back to his car. John Shepherd must hear titters every time he rang his suppliers to place an order. I'd change my name, Nick thought. Or, better, I'd open a shop selling walking gear. Everyone else in Ambleside did.

All the way back home he found himself devising new names for John Shepherd's shop. As he got to the Grasmere roundabout, another one came to him: Wool you still love me tomorrow?

Chapter 9

It was Monday, and Molly had chosen mauve. She had a cigarette half-smoked smouldering in an ash-tray and was peering in a preoccupied way at her screen.

"Morning Nick." She didn't look up.

"Hello Molly," Nick replied. It was a little after nine, but as usual Molly gave the impression of already having been at work several hours. "Much going on?" he asked her.

"Busy. Sometime I want you to check a story about more funding cuts at the National Park. We've had an internal report leaked. Sounds bloody over there. By the way, you working on anything much at the moment?"

"Well, I'm still following up the Bowfell fell race story."

"?"

"Davie Peters, the runner who died."

"Oh yes." Molly sounded uninterested. That was last week. Journalists had a notorious inability to remember anything which wasn't the immediate focus of their attention.

Nick settled himself in front of his terminal, and checked through the emails that had come in over the weekend. A waft of tobacco smoke reached him, and he instinctively coughed.

"Mmm." Molly was preoccupied. "By the way, someone rang for you a few minutes ago. Insisted that they had to speak to you, I wasn't good enough. Couldn't make it out. Something about a gatepost destroyed. Front page lead I'm thinking. The details are on that notepad by your keyboard." She hadn't looked up.

Nick looked at the note, which had a name, a phone number and the name of a village the other side of the M6 beyond Kendal. "Bit outside our circulation area, isn't it?" he asked, but Molly was engrossed in her work and failed to answer. He sighed, and reached for the phone.

An elderly voice answered. "Edgar Rothbury," it said, very formally.

"It's Nick Potterton from the *Cumbrian Enquirer* here. I think you rang for me?"

"I beg your pardon, who is calling?"

Nick repeated himself.

"Ah yes, are you the gentleman who writes the articles?" the voice enquired.

"Well, some of them." This was not going to be speedy, Nick realised.

Edgar Rothbury launched into a long tale, which Nick struggled to follow. It was, as Molly had implied, about a gatepost. Or, rather no, it was about a garden gate. It was of wrought iron, and had cost Mr Rothbury a lot of money, over five hundred pounds, that was seven years ago, it would cost much more than that now. Specially made, it had been. The design included thistles, because Edgar Rothbury's wife was from Scotland. Glenrothes.

Nick stopped taking notes. "I'm sorry, Mr Rothbury, I can't quite see why you're telling me this."

Edgar Rothbury paused momentarily. "But it's destroyed. He destroyed it. I'll never be able to get it properly mended."

"I'm very sorry." Sometimes you had to humour people.

"He gave me his phone number, but all I get is a woman's voice. Perhaps he gave me a wrong number."

Nick sighed, and decided he had to ask the question. "Who?"

"The man you wrote about. Last week, you wrote an article and it had a picture. That was him. I'd recognise him anywhere."

Light was slowly dawning. "Ah, I'm with you. The chap from Penrith." Nick had covered the case of a twenty-something man who had been hauled before the magistrates after a drunken vandalism escapade.

"No, no, no." Mr Rothbury sounded irritated. "Of course it wasn't him. It was the other man. The man you said had died. The runner."

"The fell-runner?"

"Yes. He destroyed my garden gate. He said he'd fix it, but he never did."

You got them sometimes, callers like this. Ironic, though, given how much Davie Peters had been occupying Nick's thoughts that this man had happened to choose that story. Davie Peters, international athlete and garden gate vandal, that would be a headline to conjure with. Nick started to wind up the conversation.

"Thank you *very much* for letting us know. And I'm so sorry about the gate."

But Mr Rothbury was not to be easily silenced.

"He should never have been driving a lorry that big along my road. It's a tiny country lane."

"A lorry." Nick decided to reach for the notepad after all.

"A great big white lorry, full of something, god knows what. I'd seen it on the lane before, of course."

"You're absolutely sure the driver was the person in the photograph?" Nick quizzed.

"Oh yes," Edgar Rothbury replied.

"When was this exactly?"

"It was a Sunday morning, two or three weekends back. I was out in the front garden pruning the shrubs, so he had to stop."

Nick pondered. There must be hundreds of young men in their twenties in Cumbria who drove large white lorries. Well, tens, anyway. This was almost certainly going to be another case of home-made scones and tea, with nothing to show for it at the end. On the other hand, maybe he had to at least meet the man.

"Let me come and see the gate for myself," Nick found himself saying. "How would this afternoon do?"

"Oh no, I couldn't possibly see you today. I always go to Kirkby Stephen on a Monday afternoon. My wife and I have a cup of tea and change our library books."

Mr Rothbury couldn't do Tuesday, either. The septic tank was due to be emptied, but he didn't know exactly when the men were coming. It would have to be Wednesday. At 9.30 in the morning. No scones this time then, Nick thought. He took the address details and the directions. It would be a job for the sat nav.

Nick rang off and reached across for the report about the National Park Authority Molly had mentioned. His phone rang again. He sighed.

"Hi Nick."

"Lindsay! How was your weekend? Do any cycling yesterday?"

"Phil and I cycled out to the Roman museum at Senhouse. First time I'd been there. Interesting. And an amazing view across the Solway Forth to the Galloway hills. But anyway, I've got some news and since you're a journalist I thought you'd be the person to share it with."

It was Friday night gossip from the girls' night out, and it was the one bit of gossip which Nick had asked Lindsay to try to elicit.

"So anyway, apparently they split up about a month ago," Lindsay was saying. "It was Karen who'd heard this, by the way."

Pauline hadn't lied to him when she'd said that Davie didn't have a girlfriend. At the time he died. But she certainly hadn't told him the full story.

"Does Karen know her name? Or anything else about her?"

"No, although she's pretty sure her surname was Smith."

Nick's heart sank. Smith! Why couldn't the girlfriend have had a name like Featherstonehaugh, where he'd have had a sporting chance of tracking her down?

"Karen thought her first name might be Sue or Sarah or Sandra, something like that. And she was a potter maybe. Or a wood-carver."

"That's all?"

"Sorry, that's all. But I know you, you're a newshound, you'll sniff out all the details."

"Thanks for your confidence in me, Lindsay. Fancy a drink sometime, by the way?"

"Bit busy this week. Going swimming with a couple of others tonight, though. Interested?"

"Not really. I haven't yet got this obsession with triathlons which the rest of you suddenly have."

"OK, see you as usual on Thursday anyway." She rang off.

Nick knew where his priorities lay, and it shouldn't be with the Davie Peters feature. Molly had a paper to get together by Wednesday tea time and he had stories to contribute.

Nevertheless, he couldn't resist the temptation. He remembered writing a piece a year or so back about a website service for craftspeople in Cumbria which the county council had originally set up. He found the web address easily and searched the online directory. Nothing came up that was relevant. Next he searched the national Crafts Council website. As he had expected, there were plenty of craftsmen and women called Smith. There were jewellers and fashion designers, glassmakers and enamellers, and there were even a few ceramicists and wood-carvers too, though none anywhere near the Lake District. Nick tried putting a few combinations into Google, based on combinations of Cumbria, Lake District, potter, wood-carver, crafts and Smith. Nothing at all promising came back.

Finally, as a joke, he stuck in "Davie Peters" and "girlfriend". Some Google algorithm somewhere must have laughed heartily, and thrown back at him a load of irrelevant rubbish. He rather absently changed "girlfriend" to "craftswoman" and suddenly found himself glued to his screen. There was just one Google entry, but that was enough.

Her name was Sally Smyth and she was, the article said, a craftswoman and sculptor who made objects out of Cumbrian slate. She'd been asked to carve something to be given as first prize in a local fell race over near Millom the previous year and had come up with the idea of carving the head of a Herdwick ram, the breed of sheep most associated with the high Lakeland fells. She had turned up on the race day to give it in person to the winning runner. Davie Peters of course. So that's how they'd met.

All this was recounted in a news clipping of no more than six sentences from one of the *Enquirer*'s rival newspapers based in Carlisle, which fortunately had chosen to put the story online. Six sentences were enough. Sally Smyth's own website was easy to track down when you knew her name and although it was one of those sites which is permanently under construction (probably done for her by a friend as a favour and never properly finished off) it did show four grainy photos of examples of her work, a photo of her in her studio and, amazingly, wonderfully, a contact address and mobile phone number. Nick felt that this was one of those moments when you should punch the air in triumph. He didn't, of course – Molly would have peered across at him in bewilderment and asked what was up. But he did allow himself a small smirk of pleasure.

And then he rang the number.

In hindsight, he knew he'd made a mistake. In fact, he knew the second he terminated the call. By then, though, it was too late. He'd got Sally's answerphone. She sounded young but also confident. Sally Smyth here, her message said: she pronounced her surname Smith, not Smythe. I'm not in at the moment, but please leave a message if you are interested in my work. Bye.

This was the point, Nick realised later, when he had three options. He could have hung up and tried again. He could have left a message, giving his name and phone number, and saying something like, "I'm really interested in buying one of your works for my wife's birthday, please ring me."

Or he could have left a message which explained why he was actually trying to reach her. He did this. As he started speaking, he knew for a firm fact that Sally would not be returning his call.

Most journalists have ethics. Oh yes, victims of the worst excesses of tabloid journalism may laugh a hollow laugh, but nevertheless the National Union of Journalists has an ethical code of conduct for its members, which says that journalists are to obtain material by honest, straightforward and open means. Subterfuge is allowable only for investigations that are overwhelmingly in the public interest.

There would have been occasions in his professional past when Nick would have invoked this second part of the clause to justify what he was doing. Investigative journalism sometimes seemed to demand nothing but subterfuge. But at that time in his life he had been after big fish. Now he was working for the *Cumbrian Enquirer*, and trying to get to speak to the ex-girlfriend of a Cumbrian fell-runner was hardly what the NUJ meant by overwhelming public interest.

He turned back bad-temperedly back to his screen as a large mauve cloud moved in his direction. "Nick, when you've done the National Park could you follow this up. An eighty year old OAP in Shap's had her electricity disconnected, even though she says she paid the bill. She's making do with candles. Don't say I don't give you all my juiciest leads." She thoughtfully turned her head aside to take a puff on her cigarette. "Afraid I need it as soon as possible."

Nick nodded. Journalism was the art of the possible. The art of whatever it was possible to do in a rush.

Chapter 10

There'd been a time when Sally had felt that Davie Peters was the best thing that had ever happened to her.

When they'd first met, Davie had been fired up with the success that comes from winning a race, oozing confidence and an animal physicality which she had found very attractive. He'd taken the prize from her – a little slate carving, which she'd been working on for a couple of weeks, and which she'd felt particularly pleased with – and had given her a kiss on the cheek as he did. He was still wearing his running kit, still sweaty. And then he'd smiled a mischievous smile at her.

She'd loved it the first time they'd had sex. She'd loved undressing him slowly, one article of clothing at a time, seeing his body emerge naked. She'd loved running her hands over his body, over his tight stomach, his nipples, and then feeling his muscles which were there beneath the skin. His thighs were strong and hard.

And in exchange he had explored her body, gently and patiently. He had kissed her hands, exclaiming on their roughness. It was, she had told him, what you had to put up with if you wanted to sleep with someone who was a sculptor. He'd laughed, and said there was nothing wrong with earning an honest living by the toil of your hands. She'd laughed in her turn in response.

They'd stayed in the bed for ages. He'd told her things about his life. He'd told her how he loved the Cumbrian fells, but how he loved them most of all when he was running over them. His body needed to feel the sensation which came when he ran. There was that wonderful natural high you experienced. It was much more than simple pleasure or enjoyment, he said.

"As good as an orgasm?" she had responded.

He had smiled. "Different." As if on cue, their bodies moved towards each other again.

And then she had talked about her life, and the passion she felt for her art. She had gravitated early on at art college towards sculpture, and in particular to working in stone. She loved the feel and toughness of stone, the stubbornness with which it could resist you as you tried to tease out the shapes you wanted from within it. It was a difficult material, but infinitely rewarding.

So she had surprised herself, she said, when, after she had moved from Liverpool to Cumbria, she had begun to experiment with slate. She had read up on the history of the Lake District's slate industry, had done the tourist trip round the one remaining slate mine at Honister and had fossicked around the piles of waste slate which you came across all over the Lakes, looking for pieces she could work with. Slate's softness made it in some respects easier to work with, but paradoxically that also made it very much harder to achieve the effect you wanted.

"There are very few artists really using slate imaginatively. Most of the stuff that's being made is awful tourist tat," she told Davie, who nodded.

"That Herdwick you did is nice," he said.

"You're obliged to say that," she laughed, reaching across to stop his mouth with her hand whilst with her other hand on his chest she pinned him to the bed. He accepted the restraint, making noises with his mouth as if in reply. And then he broke free, and in turn took hold of Sally. "Have I told you yet another thing about me, which is that I like to get what I want?" he said, with a smile. "And right at this moment what I want is you."

He was as good a lover as a runner, Sally thought. She wouldn't ask yet where he had gained this experience, Davie would no doubt choose to tell her in due course. For the time being she was content to know that his body was enjoying her body, and that hers in response was enjoying his.

They kept their separate lives as their relationship developed. She'd been across to see him race a few times, but had chosen to avoid getting too closely involved in his running club. She'd also steadfastly refused to have anything to do with the idea of running herself. She had hated PE and sport at school, and had no intention of changing her mind now. In turn, Davie hadn't really got involved with her own friends.

But in those first few weeks of Autumn, the passion of the new relationship had swept over them both like a wave. Sometimes they met up in Davie's upstairs flat in Ambleside. More often, Davie would come across to the little rented place she had in Cleator Moor, the former mining town where prices were still low enough for her also to be able to rent a disused builder's yard for her studio space. Davie would sometimes watch her as she worked, crunching his trainers on the waste slate chippings which she discarded and which lay about the yard.

In due course, she'd met his parents, at a Sunday dinner they'd invited her to at their house. Like Davie they lived in Ambleside. Davie's sister had been there too. The meal had not been without its difficulties (Davie's mum had seemed a little intimidated at the idea that Sally was an *artist*, whilst his dad had been unforthcoming). Sally liked Pauline very much, though. They'd a common interest in the history of the Lake District's slate industry, she rapidly discovered. Pauline was knowledgeable about the story of iron ore mining around Cleator Moor too. It was a town with quite a past, Pauline said. The mining companies had relied on migrant workers in the nineteenth century, bringing in labourers from Ireland. At one time the town had the nickname Little Ireland.

Sally and Davie had spent New Year's Eve together at Sally's place with a bottle of champagne and some DVDs. They had barely even seen midnight in. Davie had come up with some card game where you had to bet the items of clothing you were wearing. Predictably Sally found herself down to her bra and knickers before Davie had even lost his jeans, and a few moments later she was standing on her living room carpet, completely naked, facing Davie who was grinning at her.

"So what happens now?" she said.

"I think you know," he replied. He pulled off his remaining clothes himself and they dived for the bedroom. "Happy New Year," he'd said.

"Happy New Year," she had replied. They had woken the following morning in each other's arms, without even the obligatory New Year hangover.

But it hadn't been a happy new year. Not at all.

In hindsight, she perhaps should have seen the warning signs earlier than she did. Davie's drive and determination is what had attracted her to him, that aspect of his character which drove him on when he was taking part in a race in order to ensure that he was the first runner back. But that determination to win sometimes came out in other ways, too. When he had decided he wanted something he did everything he could to make sure he got it, at almost any cost. It could distort his judgement. And it could lead him to exploit his friends.

It was true, she had felt badly exploited at the end. Not sexually – he remained sensitive towards her to the last, and it had been the sex which had kept her with him for so long – but in other ways. During the summer holidays, when she had still hoped that their relationship had a future, she'd even taken to talking things through with Pauline. Considering that Pauline was Davie's sister, she had been remarkably understanding. Maybe the reason was that they shared something else apart from their common interest in Lakeland slate: towards the end, Davie had been exploiting Pauline too.

Sally had broken off with him at the start of September. But she had still hoped that maybe, just maybe, it wasn't the definitive end. She still believed that somehow she could get her original Davie back, the Davie with the passion for life that she had loved. So the news of his death had completely traumatised her. There was unfinished business here which, she realised with a desperate heart, could now never reach any sort of resolution.

In those dark dark days immediately after... after Davie's death, she had conducted a stock-check of her own life. She was living in grotty accommodation in an economically depressed town which not even its strongest advocates would describe as pretty. The savings she had managed to accumulate over the past few years with quite a lot of difficulty (she had not taken holidays, she had lived a pretty abstemious life) had now gone completely. She had to face the fact that, in a very few weeks, she would probably have to give up the studio and register as unemployed.

She'd done what so many of her contemporaries from art college had done: lived more or less on the poverty line as she committed herself to her art and tried to make the break-through into commercial recognition and success. Some people were talented or lucky and managed it. Some, equally talented, failed. Now four years after graduating, aged 26, it looked as if success wasn't going to happen for her.

Yes, she'd sold a few pieces, and she'd got a few commissions. People had told her they liked her work. She'd been promised space to exhibit in a craft fair in Keswick the weeks before Christmas, where she could probably count on selling a few more pieces – though unfortunately only at very low prices. Really, given the amount of work which even a relatively small slate piece took her, she should be charging several hundred pounds for everything she made. Mostly at the moment her work sold for somewhere around £40.

But even for the meagre pickings which Keswick would offer she needed to have things to sell, and in the days after Davie had died she had found it impossible to get back to her work. She'd tried to complete an elaborate abstract piece which she had designed primarily as a garden feature, but she hadn't concentrated. The slate had cracked. In despair, she had thrown the pieces to the ground. The dust that had risen back towards her represented two weeks' labour.

Being a self-employed artist was tough at the best of times, and this was not the best of times. She'd spent the weekend back with old friends in Liverpool, trying to get away from things, but for the first time hadn't enjoyed their company. And now it was Monday again, and the world was supposed to be working. She took herself out to the studio and attempted to find something to do. She swept up the discarded slate into a pile at the corner of the yard. She then turned her attention to the unworked slate she had recently selected, stacking the pieces together by order of size so that she could tell at a glance which pieces would be right for future projects. If there were to be future projects.

Her mobile rang, from a landline number she didn't recognise. She let it ring until the answerphone message cut in. It would be Harrods commissioning her to deliver forty large pieces for them to sell. It would be the V&A, offering her a solo exhibition. No, it wouldn't be.

When she eventually listened to the message, she discovered that it was a journalist ringing up to ask her to talk to him about Davie. What a relief she hadn't instinctively answered. Talking to a journalist about anything at the moment was the last thing she wanted. Talking about Davie was out of the question.

She took two dirty coffee cups back to the kitchen to be washed up.

And then the bloody journalist rang again. This time he came through from a mobile number, and she made the mistake of answering it. Immediately he had introduced himself she pressed the red disconnect button on her own mobile. She sat down. She found to her astonishment that she was shaking all over.

Her phone rang again and again at intervals as the day wore on. She knew without answering that it was the same man again. Eventually, she could bear it no longer. She typed out a short message, and sent it back. And then, head in hands, she sat on a kitchen chair, feeling like crying.

She was in that state of mind where she felt everything was too much. She felt physically and mentally unable to do anything other than barely exist. Depression. She knew she needed to talk to someone. She picked up her mobile again and this time selected a number already stored in the handset. It was a number which she had rung several times in the past few weeks.

Nick read Sally's text message just as he was leaving work. It had been a frustrating day all round. Molly had been in a difficult mood, and her smoking had really got to him. Or maybe it had been the other way round, and it wasn't Molly but him who had been in a mood. Either way, he was still cross at how he had blown the girlfriend contact. When he had got through, she'd put the phone down on him. And then, rightly or wrongly, he'd tried a few more times. Each time the call had gone through to the answering message.

And now here was a text reply: **I don't want to talk to you. Stop ringing. Stop this harassment**.

There was no name, but there didn't need to be. And there was a finality to the message which brooked no further attempts by him to make contact.

Nick juggled the phone between his hands, sighed, and then punched out another number. This time, the call was quickly answered.

"Lindsay? It's Nick. About this swimming tonight. Where are you meeting?"

Chapter 11

Rosa rang late on Wednesday afternoon, taking Nick by surprise as he was making a pot of tea.

"Hello, Dad," she said.

"Rosa, good to hear you. You all right?" Nick had meant to ring her, as he often did, at the weekend. Somehow, though, the days had come and gone and he hadn't got round to it. Too much going on at the moment.

"Absolutely fine. Been out running today?"

"I have, as it happens. Just a short training run. Twenty miles," he fibbed.

"I assume it's raining." The very first time Rosa had visited him in the Lakes, the weather had been atrocious. Ever since then she had teased him about the climate he had chosen when moving from London.

"Glorious sunshine, actually. Isn't it the same in London?" In fact, it had been a cheerless grey October day, albeit dry.

"What a pity I don't believe you, Dad. Look, I know this is short notice, but I was wondering what you were doing the weekend after next. I was thinking about coming up on the train."

"It would be wonderful to see you. You, and Becky as well I hope?"

"Sorry, just me. Becky's planning to go and see her parents."

"OK. I'll come across in the car and meet you at Oxenholme." Oxenholme, a small village outside Kendal, was the nearest main-line station for the Lakes, where trains stopped to connect with the branch line to Kendal and Windermere.

"Great. By the way, Becky bought me some proper walking boots for my birthday, and I need to try them out. I am relying on you to take me into the hills. Somewhere very beautiful."

"I'll see what I can devise. A day on the hills and then a meal somewhere on Saturday evening?"

"Nothing too fancy."

"I'll book a table."

"*Molt bé*." Rosa had changed language, using words which once upon a time she had used to her two parents at home in Kentish Town. It was the phrase Catalan speakers used to signal agreement. It meant fine, good, OK.

"Rosa, the Lake District is an English-speaking zone. I'm not your mother." But Nick had laughed nonetheless.

Rosa had said her goodbyes and rung off, and Nick had turned back to the kettle. Rosa's visit would be just what he needed. He'd take her onto the beautiful Kentmere fells, following the ridge of the hills along to Yoke and High Street and then on to Mardale Ill Bell. No, they'd tackle Helvellyn. Or maybe the Fairfield horseshoe would be better, they could do that from his own front door in Grasmere. Well, anyway, he'd decide something. Of course, it depended on the weather.

After the frustrations of Monday, Tuesday had been a more productive day. Molly had had a lunch appointment with a contact so that Nick had time free from distraction to polish off some of the work he'd failed to tackle on the Monday. The National Park story was finished in no time at all. The pensioner with the candles had given him a great interview on the phone, and that was written up too. He'd subbed the bulk of the contributions which, as always, had been piling up in his email box from the voluntary correspondents which the *Enquirer* recruited in each town and village across its patch. He was busy. It meant the Davie Peters story had been untouched.

But today had been the day when he had made the appointment with Mr and Mrs Rothbury. The great garden gate affair. He got up in good time to make sure he arrived as arranged at 9.30.

He extricated himself from the Rothburys' bungalow after two hours, not without some difficulty. Edgar Rothbury was the same as he had been on the phone, only more so. His wife Betty, it immediately became clear, was not well. Nick wasn't an expert, but it seemed to him pretty clearly dementia. Edgar was probably desperate for Nick's company and conversation.

Even with the sat nav, Nick had nearly been late. As Edgar had told him on the phone, the bungalow was indeed up a narrow country lane, one of a maze of similar lanes in the limestone countryside west of Kirkby Stephen in the far south-east corner of Cumbria. Walkers walking the Coast to Coast route passed a little to the south; round here, though, there seemed to be no footpaths and nobody at all about.

The bungalow dated back perhaps to the 1930s. The Rothburys had bought it ten years or so earlier, Edgar said, shortly after he had retired. They had been living in Preston and he had worked for British Aerospace, BAe as they called it now, as a draftsman. He and Betty had loved driving out into the countryside at weekends, and when he got his pension they took the decision to move. The bungalow was in a beautiful location, he said.

It was indeed. But Nick reckoned that Edgar and Betty Rothbury had almost certainly not thought about the other aspects of living there. There was no passing traffic of any kind and there was also a slight eeriness about the area which Nick found unsettling. He wouldn't have wanted to live there himself and he began to wonder just how safe it was for two pensioners to be living alone in such an isolated spot. He had asked Edgar about neighbours, and Edgar had in reply mumbled something about two or three farms further up the lane. To Nick's amazement, he didn't appear to know who lived there. This, he thought, is the rural idyll in reality. Ten years in, and you still don't know the neighbours.

No wonder the Rothburys' garden was important to the couple. And their poor garden gate. It had certainly met a sticky end. Edgar was frustratingly vague: it had been a big lorry, which had come round the bend from the direction of the main road too fast and gone straight into it. He had seen the lorry the previous Sunday, too, several times. It had been a white sort of colour.

"It had had canvas sides, so I couldn't see what was inside," Edgar said. He paused. "Do you think it could have been a badger baiter? I've heard that people do that."

Nick laughed. "I don't think badger baiters go out with heavy goods vehicles. Did you take a note of the numberplate?"

No, Edgar Rothbury hadn't written down the registration number. However he was adamant of one thing: the identity of the driver. It was the man in your photograph, he told Nick. And then, when Nick had tried to question him further: Of course I'm sure. Are you doubting my word?

Davie Peters was not, however, the name which the driver had left with Edgar Rothbury. According to the piece of paper which Edgar produced from an old-fashioned bureau in the bungalow's lounge, the driver that day had been someone by the name of Rowan Atkinson. Edgar had appeared not to find anything unlikely about this, and had certainly not asked for any proof of identity. Well, Nick thought, there could indeed be a Cumbrian truck driver called Rowan Atkinson. At least the note hadn't said Charlie Chaplin.

"What about the phone number?" Nick asked, looking at the mobile number written beneath.

"I've tried it twice. It was a woman's voice on a message. I don't think her name was Atkinson."

"OK, tell you what, I'll ring it myself from the *Enquirer*'s office and see who I get," Nick said, starting to write down the number in his notebook.

He got no further than the first three digits when, with a sudden shock, he realised that the number was one which was familiar to him. He stopped, and suddenly felt weak. It was the phone number of Sally Smyth.

It didn't make sense. And there was another thing which Nick was struggling to understand. When he had finally prised himself from Edgar Rothbury's clutches and left the bungalow, he hadn't driven back down the lane to the main road but instead had turned the other way. He wanted to find out why anyone driving a large truck, whether they were called Rowan Atkinson, Davie Peters or anything else, would conceivably bring it up past the Rothburys' bungalow.

He was prepared to discount badger baiting, but was unable to come up with any explanation more plausible. About half a mile further up the lane, there was an old stone farmhouse on the left hand side, with a farm yard and barn alongside. Nick stopped the car, and rang the door. Nobody in. He walked into the farmyard and called out, but it was obvious nobody was there. Not even a dog barked. A sheep farm with the farmer out on the fells perhaps, Nick thought.

Beyond here the tarmac ran out, and the lane changed into a rough farm track. He drove on, and found himself after a few minutes at another farm. The building would definitely have not appealed to any retired couples from Preston wanting to move to the country: although made of local stone, it seemed to cower under a dark limestone scar of rock which rose up behind it, so that even in the middle of an October day there was little light to enjoy. It was in a terrible state of repair. Two of the downstairs windows had been patched with thick plastic film, and there were weeds growing beside the front door. Alongside was a series of farm buildings, again half-derelict, and beyond them in turn a graveyard for old vehicles, parked in what appeared to be an old quarry closed off by a couple of strands of loose barbed wire. And next to the quarry, parked on a patch of rough tarmac, were a Land Rover and a mechanical digger, its long neck hanging limply over the whole sorry scene. The Land Rover did, however, have a current road tax, Nick noticed.

Despite appearances, the farm was obviously lived in. Two dogs were chained up in the yard, and their barking rose to a frenzy as Nick cautiously left his car and hammered on the front door. But at this farm, too, nobody was in. With some relief, Nick hurried back to his own vehicle. Cities had some terrible areas, which good folk trembled to visit. But what city dwellers didn't realise was that the countryside, too, had areas like that. Just as run-down, and just as unwelcoming.

The track where he had parked was wet and he was struggling to open the driver's door whilst avoiding the puddles when he noticed the tyre marks in the mud. Some vehicle with very large tyres had been this far up the track, and recently, too. Hmm. He noted down mentally the name which hung on an old sign: Under Cragg Farm.

Nick turned the car and headed back towards the main road home, taking the bend past the Rothburys' bungalow with care. Once again he thought how lonely it must be to live there. He hoped that social services knew of the couple and kept an eye on them.

He stopped the car in Ambleside. It was lunchtime, and he felt both tired and hungry. He decided to go to a café that had opened a year or two previously just off Ambleside's main street. It was above a climbing shop, and the clientele was strongly outdoorsy in its orientation. Nick ordered a sandwich and a mug of tea, found a quiet table where he could work and got out his laptop. He'd arranged with Molly to write up the Rothbury story immediately after the interview and send it through to the office. He hadn't banked on being with them quite so long, but there were still a couple of hours before the news pages were finally put to bed. He began typing.

Two Cumbrian pensioners have been left heart-broken after a callous lorry-driver destroyed their valuable wrought-iron garden gate.

It was not difficult to write this sort of stuff in the way people wanted, Nick thought. Some student on a media course somewhere would be able to deconstruct his technique easily enough: the way he'd slipped in emotionally laden words like heart-broken and callous, for example, and the fact that he'd deliberately called the Rothburys pensioners. The alternative would have been 'retired couple', but 'pensioners' somehow sounded more needy, more likely to be victims of a cruel world, or at least a cruel conman.

Nick quickly spelled out the bones of the story: where the Rothburys lived, what had happened, why it mattered so much to them. He mentioned how they had selected the design, including the thistle motif, "chosen to remind Betty Rothbury of her beloved homeland of Scotland". He popped the first quote into the third paragraph:

"It cost us hundreds and hundreds of pounds. We will never be able to replace it now," said Edgar Rothbury, looking at the mangled metal remains at the end of his garden drive.

And then on to the lorry and its driver.

When confronted, the driver claimed that his name was Rowan Atkinson and left a false mobile phone number. He was described by Mr Rothbury as white, in his twenties and of athletic build.

That was the nearest Nick could get to anything linking the story with Davie, of course. No newspaper could run with Edgar Rothbury's uncorroborated assertion that he had recognised the driver from the previous week's edition: the story wasn't properly stood up, as journalists would say. Potentially libellous, too. Instead, Nick ended with a final quote:

Edgar Rothbury said that he had seen the lorry, which he described as a white heavy goods vehicle with closed curtain sides, several times before in his lane. "He shouldn't have been driving here at all. It's a No Through Road. I've no idea what he thought he was doing," he said.

Nick stopped typing, went to 'Tools' and selected 'Word Count'. 232 words. Good, just right. He'd told Molly to expect something between 200 and 250 words. He connected the laptop to his mobile network and sent the story on its way, straight to Molly's personal email at the *Enquirer*.

And then he decided to treat himself to a second cup of tea and a flapjack, and began mulling over once again where the Davie Peters story was taking him. It was time to talk to the parents, he decided. He'd been meaning to try to interview Pa Peters, as Detective Inspector Mulholland called him, and his wife for some time but hadn't yet got round to it. He had found their address in Ambleside without any difficulty in the phone directory and had also noticed that Gary Peters had a further entry in the Yellow Pages. Gary Peters Haulage, he called himself.

Their house was no more than ten minutes' walk away from the town centre. It was a 1950s semi at the northern end of the town with the former garden beside it turned into an extensive yard, protected by a large padlocked metal gate. Behind, just squeezed in with only inches to spare, was Mr Peters' wagon. It was, to Nick's inexperienced eye, a big beast, with two sets of four tyres at the back and a further set of four tyres under the cab at the front. It was cream, or off-cream, rather than white, and it had been left unloaded, with the curtains which made up its sides right pulled back. Nick surreptitiously took a couple of photos of it with his phone's camera. And then he turned, and made for the front door.

His timing was unfortunate. If he had foregone the flapjack and turned up, say, twenty minutes earlier, he would have found Margaret Peters puffed from her bike ride back from work but prepared to talk to him. She was a regular reader of the *Enquirer* and had faithfully kept all the reports which the paper had published of Davie's achievements as a junior cross-country runner. She had also cut out Nick's piece the previous week on Davie's death, which although she had found it almost too painful to read was, she felt, a fair report of what had happened. What's more, with Gary away, off for a day's fishing for tench and carp at little Cleabarrow Tarn near

Windermere, she would have not been in a particular hurry to get food on the table. Nick would almost certainly have been invited in, and offered a cup of tea.

But Nick arrived too late. A distraught Margaret Peters answered the front door, barely even listened to him as he introduced himself, and immediately slammed the door back in his face.

The door-stepping score was now Fifteen-all with the Peters family, Nick thought ruefully. Fifteen-thirty if you added in the brush-off he had had from Sally Smyth on Monday.

Perhaps, had he known, Nick would ideally have arrived not twenty but ten minutes earlier. If he had, he would have seen a black Land Rover Discovery draw up a few doors away down the street. He would have seen a man, in his late thirties or early forties, emerge from the vehicle and make his way to the Peters' front door. He would have noticed that the man was dressed in a suit, and was carrying in his right hand a somewhat battered black briefcase. He would have seen him ring the bell. He would have seen the door open. He would have seen the man introduce himself, would have seen Margaret Peters' cautious response, would have seen her reject the bundle of papers which the man had reached for from his briefcase. He would have overheard the argument which ensued. And, finally, he would have seen the man walk away from the front door. Telling Mrs Peters that he would be back.

But when Nick arrived the Peters' road was empty and the Land Rover Discovery gone. All that was left for him to discover was a woman on the edge of tears, who appeared to be both furious and frightened at the same time and who was definitely, categorically, not going to talk to him or anyone else about her son.

Chapter 12

"Mr Rothbury might have been right: perhaps it had been Davie driving the lorry that Sunday. OK, so Davie was wrong to give a false name, but still, it was only a gate he'd damaged."

Lindsay was working things out aloud, talking to Nick as he drove out of Kendal on the quiet A-road to Tebay and Kirkby Stephen. It was Friday afternoon, and they'd agreed over the usual drinks the evening before to go out for a training run together. Technically, Nick should have been working, but he'd told himself that this was *almost* work. Lindsay had no such problems: Fridays were one of her free days.

"And perhaps Sally Smyth's phone number had been the first one that had come to mind when he had to give a number?" Lindsay went on.

"Possibly. I've wondered whether he'd done it to spite her. To make her have to cope with endless phone calls from an incoherent elderly gent complaining about a gate," Nick responded.

Nick had told Lindsay in the pub what he knew about Sally Smyth, partly because Lindsay had asked what he had found out and he was uncomfortable at the idea of fobbing her off. He had then added a little bit about his encounter with the Rothburys. If he was honest, he wanted somebody else's opinion of what it might all mean.

"Out of spite? I suppose it could have been a really nasty bust-up." Lindsay was still pondering Nick's last suggestion.

"Or, hang on, maybe Sally left Davie to go off with a new boyfriend," she went on. "Who has now moved in with her. The boyfriend's using Sally's phone number at the moment, and he was the man who damaged the garden gate. So the number was genuine."

Nick was watching the road carefully for any errant sheep that might have wandered off the fells on to the carriageway. "Let me get this right, Lindsay. You're saying that Sally Smyth dumped Davie and took up immediately with another person who, at least according to

Mr Rothbury, is the spitting image of Davie and who, what's more, also happens to drive a white lorry. Bit of a coincidence maybe?"

"I agree it sounds a little implausible. But just because things seem unlikely doesn't necessarily mean they don't happen. I went out with a mathematician once – this was long before Greg – and he tried to explain probability theory to me. Did you know that if you have 23 people in a room together, there's a fifty/fifty chance that two of them will share a birthday? It's true."

"I'll take your word for it. Don't forget my degree was history."

The story of the Rothburys' garden gate had appeared in the latest issue of the *Enquirer* exactly as he had written it. He had picked up the paper as usual that morning at the Grasmere newsagents and had read it over breakfast. Molly had decided to run it as the page five lead, Nick noticed. Same spot two weeks running. Coincidence, of course.

And now Nick was retracing the route he had driven two days earlier when he was researching that piece, back to the quiet country lane where the Rothburys had their bungalow. It had been Lindsay's idea. Nick had said that he wanted to go back to have another look at what might lie up the lane, and Lindsay had suggested they combine it with a run. It wouldn't look like snooping about. What could be more normal than a pair of runners heading off into the countryside?

"Not long now," he said to Lindsay. They had just crossed over the M6 and were arriving at the roundabout by the motorway exit at Tebay. "The turn's a few miles further on."

"My theory is that Davie, or Sally's new boyfriend, or Rowan Atkinson or whoever it was, was just dropping off building supplies. Somebody's putting up a new farm building," Lindsay said after a moment's silence. "Did you see anything like that last time?"

"Nothing."

"Gas pipes. Maybe they're laying gas pipelines."

"Didn't see any," Nick responded.

He turned off the main road, pointing out the Rothburys' bungalow to Lindsay as he drove past it. "Hmm, I see what you mean about that gate," she had replied. They'd continued up the lane, passing the next farm beyond it and on, beyond where the tarmac stopped. Nick pulled in off the track beside the mechanical digger which was still parked where it had been, a few metres before Under Cragg Farm itself was reached. "Here we are. Home sweet home."

Nick admitted to himself that he was relieved not to be alone. He liked the thought that Lindsay would be there too if they came across the occupant of Under Cragg. Cumbrian farmers could sometimes be a curmudgeonly breed. And nobody would claim that the farmhouse looked welcoming.

The Under Cragg dogs were at home. The sound of loud barking began immediately he and Lindsay left the car. Fair enough, Nick thought. It was a deserted lane and, surely, nobody ever before had chosen to come here for a run. If this was their cover story, it was pretty implausible and besides which it wasn't even a nice day to be out on the hills. The drizzle which had spattered the windscreen as they'd approached Kendal had turned into proper rain, and a cold northern wind hit them as they changed in the lee of the car into their fell-running shoes.

Nick pulled out the OS map he had already looked at beforehand. A footpath was shown leaving the track between the farmhouse and the outbuildings and although it was not, of course, signed on the ground, Nick led the way, making sure that he and Lindsay kept well beyond the furthest range of the dogs and their chains. The barking rose in a wild crescendo as they jogged past.

"Hello? Anyone there?" Nick decided to get in an opening conversational gambit, just in case a shotgun and its owner were about to emerge from the back of the farm. He had a sixth sense that somebody somewhere was about, but there was no reply.

The map showed that the footpath left the rear of the farmyard to run alongside the right hand side of a boundary fence. The route was only just about clear: over a broken-down stile, blocked up with barbed wire, which they clambered over with considerable difficulty. Beyond was a large patch of stinging nettles, fortunately now dying back.

"I wouldn't choose to come this way in high summer," Nick said to Lindsay.

"I wouldn't normally choose to come this way on a wet Friday in October either," she replied.

"Should be better soon." Nick was reading the map. The light yellow colourwash on the map told him that they would shortly leave the farmland behind to arrive at open country: right-to-roam territory, part of that mass of unenclosed mountain, heath and moorland which ramblers had campaigned for so long to be open to all – or open to all who actually fancied roaming the high wilderness areas of England – and which now at last was indeed free to explore. Ten years or so earlier, before the legislation had changed, you'd have run the risk of being turned back by an irate gamekeeper or farmer. Now you had the law on your side. Though, Nick thought quietly, what would that be worth if someone did appear and accost them?

But there was nobody. Nick and Lindsay kept to the boundary edge of the field, struggling through the vegetation. Both were wearing light waterproof cagoules over their running tops and the usual black tights to cover their legs. The rain smacked into their faces. A few sheep grazed disconsolately beside them.

"I thought you said it would be getting better," Lindsay said. They paused briefly and looked around. This was a landscape which no-one could call beautiful. Humans had been this way looking to extract what wealth they could from the land, and the results of their work had definitely left their mark. To the left were a set of small worked-out quarries, similar to the one back at Under Cragg and – just like that one – also full of rusting metal farming implements of various kinds. At their feet the ground was heavily churned up with caterpillar-style tracks, so that their running shoes were caked and muddy water splashed up on to their tights as they ran. It looked as if the farmer, whoever he was, had been out with the digger, presumably clearing the field. If so, the work wasn't yet finished: light grey lumps of limestone remained, poking up out of the soil.

They laboured on, the path climbing all the time towards a distant moorside wall.

And then, quite abruptly, things *did* get better. The ground levelled out as Nick and Lindsay arrived at open country. They climbed over stone steps set in the wall and for the first time had a decent view ahead of them.

What they saw was an amazing sight. A cold grey sea spread out before them, disappearing in all directions as far as the eye could see. It was a sea made of rock.

"Wow," Lindsay said simply.

"Limestone pavement."

"I know. This must be one of the finest stretches in England. Did you know this was here? I didn't."

Nick shook his head as a reply. The landscape could not have been more different from the familiar Lakeland mountains among which they both now lived their lives. The Cumbrian fells could be harsh and hostile and needed respect, but somehow that landscape was a familiar one. This was altogether a more alien land.

Most people in England who encounter limestone pavement do so by making the effort to clamber up the popular tourist footpath to the top of Malham Cove, the horseshoe crag about fifty miles further south in the Yorkshire Dales national park which, once upon a time, was an eighty-metre high waterfall. There are guidebooks aplenty to describe what you will find there, and to introduce the particular vocabulary which goes with limestone pavements: how the flat beds of limestone have been chiselled out by millions of years of rainfall into the distinctive blocks, or clints, which now make up the pavements and how the often deep crevices between the clints carry the name of grykes, or if you prefer grikes. Smaller runnels score the pavement surfaces, channelling surface water into the grykes.

Guidebooks will have warnings, too, for walkers to take care. They will describe how, particularly in wet weather, limestone pavements can be dangerous places, with the surface limestone likely to be slippery and the deep grykes hazardous.

At Malham Cove, it's hard to choose a time when the landscape isn't crowded with visitors. By contrast, Nick and Lindsay cut solitary figures, two runners alone with the limestone. They picked their way with caution across the pavements, following where possible the faint paths that they found which ran between the clints. At one stage Nick half-caught his foot in a particularly deep crevice, and Lindsay had to put out her arms to catch him.

"Steady," she said.

"Sorry. Wasn't paying attention. I was actually looking ahead, at that little bush growing there. Is it juniper?"

"Elder, I think."

"This is a fantastically beautiful place. Weird, but beautiful."

They progressed slowly, covering perhaps half the ground that they would have been able to run in the Lakes. Nick navigated, choosing a route which took them into the very heart of the limestone pavement area. Then they swung west in a wide arc, before turning back towards the lane where Nick's car was parked. They emerged half a mile or so from Under Cragg Farm, and made their way back up the farm track.

"What a great run," Lindsay said, as they arrived back at the car.

Time had gone by, and it was already after half past five. The rain which had greeted them as they had started their run had settled into a persistent drizzle, so that it was already beginning to get dark. Under Cragg looked even less inviting than usual, though Nick noticed a light was now burning in one of the upstairs windows. The dogs had recommenced barking as they arrived.

"OK, quick change into some dry clothes, and let's be on our way," Nick said.

He pulled off his wet running top and pulled on a teeshirt and sweatshirt, and then stripped down to his underpants to replace the sodden tights with dry jeans. Lindsay went round to the far side of the vehicle and she, too, unselfconsciously stripped to her sports bra and put on the dry clothes she had packed. Nick opened both the driver's and front passenger's doors, turned the ignition and also put on the car's heater full blast. The car pulled away down the track, and Under Cragg began to disappear in the rear-view mirror.

It was perhaps fifteen or twenty seconds before Nick realised something was wrong.

"Bloody hell," he said.

"Something up?"

"Puncture, I think."

He brought the car to a halt and jumped out. There could unfortunately be no mistake. The front offside tyre was flat against the muddy surface of the track.

Lindsay had by this stage also got out.

"Have you got a spare?"

"Yes, though it's ages since I last had to change a tyre. I'm not sure I can even remember where the jack is."

Lindsay looked back down the lane to Under Cragg. "There's a light on. I could go and see if there's anyone there to help."

Nick too looked back. "No, let's leave Under Cragg alone," he said. By this stage he had extricated the jack from a cloth bag he had found in the boot and had begun to position it in place under the chassis.

"It's a bugger that I've just changed into dry clothes," he said, as he crouched beside the tyre, the damp evening rain splattering down on him. Lindsay stood beside him, beginning to shiver slightly.

As a general rule, journalists are usually good with words and rather less good at car maintenance. Nick, however, made a passable effort at the job in hand. In five minutes or so, the wheel-nuts had been loosened and the flat tyre removed, the spare put in its place and the nuts retightened. Finally, Nick ratcheted down the jack, and the car settled back down on to the mud.

"Well done," Lindsay said.

"All part of the service."

Nick turned the ignition on again, and eased the gear into first. For a second time his car began to move forward, picking up speed as Nick changed into second gear and then third. They were approaching the start of the tarmac lane and the other farmhouse had come into sight not far ahead.

And then the car began for a second time to drive in a very strange way. A nasty rumbling sound was emerging from just below the passenger's door. Nick coasted to a halt, and once again jumped out. He glanced down: there was nothing wrong with the spare tyre he had just put in place instead of the flat. He moved round to the other side of the car. It was the front nearside tyre this time which had a puncture.

Lindsay by this stage had got out of the car as well. She and Nick looked at each other, weighing up the circumstances.

"Lindsay, that old boyfriend of yours, the mathematician. What did he say was the probability of driving without a puncture for over ten years and then getting two on the same afternoon?"

Lindsay shrugged and said nothing.

"What do you think?" Nick went on. "I suppose the surface of the track is a bit rough. Maybe I drove over something?"

"I don't think that's what it was," Lindsay replied simply. They both looked back down the track, where the faint light of Under Cragg could still just be made out.

"I don't have another spare," Nick said. "I'd better ring the breakdown people."

He pulled out his mobile phone and reached inside the dashboard to find the booklet which gave the emergency number. "Damn. Absolutely no signal for the phone here. Could you check yours?"

Lindsay did as she was asked. "Sorry, Nick, I haven't got a signal either." Again they looked at each other.

"OK, well we'll just have a little bit more exercise than we planned this afternoon. Better get our cagoules back on. I'll park the car a bit better and then we'll walk down the lane until the phones work. Or if need be I could call in at the next farm and ask to use their phone."

But the farm was in darkness, and nobody came to the front door.

Lindsay laughed. "Ever had the feeling that you're not very welcome?"

Nick made a snorting noise. "The Rothburys' bungalow isn't very far ahead. I'm sure they'll be at home."

Together Nick and Lindsay continued down the lane. It was now definitely getting towards twilight, and the drizzle had once again settled back into steady rain. An occasional sheep looked up at them from the fields beside the road. Periodically, Nick checked the two mobiles: still no signal for either.

After perhaps three-quarters of a mile, the bungalow came into sight, lights blazing from almost all the windows.

"Thank god for that," Lindsay said.

Nick went through the broken garden gate and rang the front door bell. No-one came. He tried again, more insistently. After what seemed like a further interminable delay the door opened, but only a crack. The chain had been put on. Edgar Rothbury's face peered out, anxiously.

"Who's there?"

"Hello, Mr Rothbury, it's Nick here from the *Enquirer*. Sorry to trouble you again so late in the day."

"Who are you?" Edgar Rothbury repeated.

"It's Nick Potterton from the *Cumbrian Enquirer*. You remember, I was here on Wednesday."

Recognition dawned on Edgar Rothbury's face. However, far from opening the door to welcome Nick in, he seemed to recoil further into the hall.

"I can't speak to you," he said. "You must go away."

"Sorry?" Nick struggled to make sense of what he was hearing. "I just need to ask a favour. The car's broken down nearby and I need to ring the breakdown service. Would it be OK if I used your phone?"

"No, you mustn't come in," said Mr Rothbury more firmly than ever.

"Why not?"

"I mustn't talk to you."

"Why's that?"

"Because you're a journalist. He told me not to talk to the press."

"Somebody told you not to talk to me?" Nick asked. "Who? When?"

"He did. He rang me up after your article appeared, and he said it was foolish of me to allow my name to go into a newspaper. All sorts of bad people read newspapers, he said. People would know where we lived. They might come and burgle us when we were out. Or mug us when we were in, tie us up and take all our money." Edgar Rothbury paused. "Go away, you must go now."

"I'm sorry, Mr Rothbury, but you must tell me who it was who rang you. It could be important."

"It was the man who damaged the gate. Mr Atkinson. He said he was sorry he hadn't been round before but he would definitely be coming very soon to fix it."

"Mr Atkinson phoned? Rowan Atkinson?"

"Yes. And he told me all about the risks that can come from talking to the newspapers. I had never thought of it like that before."

"But I work for the *Cumbrian Enquirer*. Surely you trust us?"

"No, because you were wrong, weren't you? You said that Mr Atkinson was dead. But he's rung me up, so he obviously isn't dead. You printed a falsehood. And you even got his name wrong, you said he was called Peters."

Nick pondered how to respond. This was an occasion when reasoned argument would get you nowhere. He weighed up making one final effort to explain his predicament, and gave up.

"Of course, I'm sorry to have troubled you." He turned and headed back to the lane where Lindsay was waiting.

"All done then?" she said brightly.

"Er – not precisely. Let's keep walking."

It was Nick's mobile which picked up a signal first, after about another half hour's walking. Nick eagerly phoned through, and spoke to the operator. Of course they would be there to help, just as soon as they could. But they had an unusually large number of calls coming through just at the moment so it could be an hour and a half. Please put on the hazard lights and for safety reasons move well away from the vehicle.

"Back to the car," Nick said, as they began the long trek back along the lane. As they started off, Nick noticed that his phone was showing a voicemail message waiting for him. Someone had rung for him, at about three o'clock.

He called through to download the message. It was a voice he recognised.

"Hello, Mr Potterton. It's John Shepherd here, from the shop in Ambleside. Just to say that there are people upstairs in the flat at the moment. Two women, this time."

Chapter 13

Sally Smyth heard the letterbox close and the sound of mail falling to the floor. The postwoman in Cleator who delivered to her part of the town tended to come a little later on Saturdays, but she herself was only just in the process of getting up. Even if she was hardly finding the energy to do much work at the moment, she still treated weekends differently from weekdays and allowed herself the luxury of a late breakfast.

There was just one envelope waiting beside the front door, and it was obviously the bank statement. Sally took it over to the kitchen table, and opened it methodically. It was, she knew, not going to be good news.

She let her eye run down the row of numbers until she reached the number at the bottom of the page. This was definitely worse than she had expected. She looked back up the page and noticed that almost half the entries were from the bank itself. There were three charges made for cheques represented but marked referred to drawer. There was a charge listed as interest. And there was a very hefty charge which read simply 'Unauthorised overdraft charge'. Not surprisingly with all these debits, she was well and truly overdrawn now.

She had in times past prided herself on her careful approach to money. She had counted the pennies carefully, had made sure she had cash put aside for the household bills, had shopped at some of the cheaper supermarkets. Then, of course, one memorable afternoon almost a year ago now, she had met Davie.

It must have been February, after they'd been together for three or four months. She'd just been to the cash machine, one Saturday night. Davie had taken part in, and won, a fell race that day, and the two of them had agreed that they'd meet up later for a pizza together. He'd mentioned casually that he was a bit skint and she hadn't thought twice, pulling out her purse and handing him fifty pounds. Give it back when you can, she said. They'd sealed the agreement across the restaurant table with a brief kiss, and, later that evening, back in her place, with rather a lot more than that. She remembered the night well. He was bouncing with energy, full of life, full of the pleasures from the day's race, lying naked on his back in her bed. She was on top of him. Their bodies met together as one.

And then there had been a couple of times a little later in the Spring when she'd lent him a hundred. Or, more precisely, given him. And then, finally, the two last occasions. Five hundred the first time. 750 the next. And each time, later on, they had had sex, amazing sex. Davie had been at his kindest and most thoughtful towards her.

The idea occurred to her: if she had priced up the average cost of each of those fucks… She pushed the thought away.

Davie was no more, but Davie was still having an effect on her life. And influencing what she did with her time. Like today. She ought to get a move on, she'd need to leave the house in a couple of hours if she wasn't going to be late.

She pushed the bank statement aside and sat deep in her own thoughts. Beside her was a coffee mug, which still had a few dregs left from the pot she'd made for herself at the start of breakfast. She played with it aimlessly. And then she came to a decision. She knew, as if by a flash of illumination, what was the way forward for her. She would be saying goodbye to Davie for a final time very soon, when at long last the coroner had finished with whatever he was doing and they could hold the funeral. And that very same day, she decided, she would say a farewell to the Lake District.

Her tenancy of the place at Cleator was running out anyway very soon, so she could extricate herself from that. She would close the studio, too. She would phone the people in Keswick and tell them she couldn't display at the craft fair, and she knew for a fact that they wouldn't care one jot.

She also knew that she would never want to work again in slate – that moment in her life was over.

She would, perhaps, return to Liverpool. She needed a job, and Liverpool, with all its economic problems, would still be a better bet than Cleator. A friend from art school was working at the moment in a call centre – just until work picked up, she'd said, but they both knew what that really meant – and apparently the call centre was still recruiting. She could do that. And she'd talk to the bank first thing on Monday, try to sort things out, at least try to turn the unauthorised overdraft into an authorised one. In due course, she would pay it off. In due course, life would sort itself out. Who knows, she might even find another man. One who was solvent.

Chapter 14

Nick woke up feeling unwell. Not precisely ill, just a bit under the weather with what felt like the beginnings of a sore throat. Well, the night before probably hadn't helped. Altogether it had been a pretty damp and cold experience. He and Lindsay had in the end had to wait for the best part of two hours for the breakdown guy to turn up and sort them out. Nick had finally got back home about half past ten, had cooked himself up a poached egg – about the only thing he'd fancied by that stage – and had almost immediately gone to bed.

He looked at the alarm clock beside the bed, which showed that it was already after nine. He dragged himself to the bathroom and got the shower running. As he did, he sneezed twice. Damn, damn, a cold on the way. Just what he could have done without.

He had arranged to go to Carlisle this Saturday, for lunch. It was a date; well, it was a sort-of-date, with a woman whose name was Cheryl. They'd arranged it a fortnight or so back, at a time when his life had seemed a bit more straightforward, and he had only remembered the day before … a bloody good thing he hadn't forgotten.

Cheryl was his latest attempt to find true love – or, let's be grown-up and sensible about this, at least a companion – through the columns of a national newspaper. This time it had been the Encounters section of the Times. Cheryl had said that she liked mountain walking, and bird-watching, and French art films, and that her favourite view was the view you got of Great Gable rising up beyond Wast Water as you drove up the single track road from Nether Wasdale. That was one of his favourite views too. He could talk to her about that, and about Les Enfants de Paradis and Manon des Sources, and about the golden eagles of Haweswater. That should be enough to get things started. It might go on from there.

Perhaps what had particularly attracted him, he secretly admitted, was the fact that Cheryl lived in Carlisle. Carlisle seemed to have worked for Lindsay, who was obviously happy to have met Phil. Maybe, just maybe, Carlisle could do it for him too.

Cheryl had said to him on the phone that she really would prefer to meet him for the first time at lunchtime rather than for an evening meal out. He'd said that was fine with him, and she had told him that there was a quite nice Italian restaurant near the centre of Carlisle where she could book a table. They'd agreed to meet there at 1pm.

Nick emerged from the shower and sneezed twice more. He pondered ringing to postpone, but decided that Cheryl just might be the one he had been waiting for and it would be a pity to miss a life-changing moment just because of a slight cold. He would take a couple of paracetamol with his breakfast fruit juice.

He then pondered what he should wear. This was supposed to be important. He'd known of women who had turned up for these sorts of dates, had checked the colour of the man's socks or their shoes or something like that, and had dumped them immediately just on the basis of that. Generally he felt he scrubbed up pretty adequately when it was necessary and he would definitely have made an effort had he and Cheryl been meeting up for an evening meal. But somehow this time he couldn't be bothered. He reached for his usual weekend wear: it was a shirt, a well-worn casual jacket and jeans. He found some clean socks. He hoped it would do.

The date – if that is what you wanted to call it – got off to a lousy start. He had left Grasmere in plenty of time for the thirty or so miles of drive to Carlisle, but had encountered abnormally heavy traffic on the approach to Keswick and then again on the A595 a couple of miles south of Carlisle itself. And then he had struggled to find a parking place, among all the Saturday lunchtime shoppers. He was ten minutes late finding the restaurant. He saw Cheryl immediately, sitting by herself at a table, looking fed up. She'd probably felt she was going to be stood up.

And the atmosphere was all wrong for any attempt at intimacy. A couple of tables away, a family were enjoying a meal of pizzas together. The two parents were there with two kids, aged perhaps nine and seven, obviously to celebrate one of the children's birthdays. The children were well-behaved enough, just a bit exuberant – and a bit young.

Cheryl was pretty in a very English sort of way, with long brown hair which came down either side of her face. She'd taken rather more care than Nick as regards the dressing-up, and was wearing a cream linen shirt and over it a nicely tailored jacket and a calf-length skirt which looked expensive and not too prim. Nick felt seriously underdressed.

Cheryl seemed nervous. She had already had more time than she wanted to inspect the menu and was anxious to get the order in. She went for whitebait as a starter and then pollo alla cacciatora, which they both agreed sounded good but would turn out when it emerged from the kitchen about half an hour later to be the restaurant's way of saying chicken stew. Nick would have preferred to have skipped the starter but in the circumstances this clearly wasn't an option. He chose calamari, with sea bass to follow. They both ordered glasses of dry white wine, which arrived almost immediately. They chinked glasses. Nick stifled an incipient sneeze.

Cheryl had begun by asking Nick about his job, which was kind and thoughtful of her no doubt, but which was really not the question he would have preferred. People could have an odd idea about journalism, an old-fashioned idea of Fleet Street and eye-shades and hot metal, and – especially – the glamour of it all. Disabusing them could be hard work. Telling them that really it was just a job like any job could sound a bit like inverted snobbery. He sighed to himself silently, and made the résumé of his life's progress towards the *Cumbrian Enquirer* as short as he decently could.

"So you used to work for the Sunday Times." Cheryl was eager for more details, more information. Or maybe she was just being polite. "That must have been amazing. Did you interview anyone famous?"

"Not really, or at least no-one who's famous any more." Nick responded. "But you know, really the *Cumbrian Enquirer* is just as interesting. Closer to its readers too." He reached for his handkerchief to blow his nose. "But, tell me, you said you were interested in bird-watching. Have you ever been to the nature reserve at Geltsdale over in the Pennines? Not far from here."

Nick had interviewed the warden a few months back and felt confident that he had enough to keep the conversation going through the first course. He was right. And from there the conversation moved on to more general talk about the north Pennines.

Cheryl knew the area well. "Have you seen the amazing view across to the Lakes from the top of Cross Fell?" she asked him. Nick, suddenly feeling like a recent arrival from England's deep South, had to confess that he hadn't. He sneezed.

"Bless you," she said.

She had been widowed. She had lost her husband to testicular cancer about two years back. Nick wasn't sure, but he had a strong feeling that she was only just beginning to feel able to move on. He might very well be the first man she'd chosen to meet in this way since then. No wonder she seemed a little ill at ease. And she obviously missed Mark terribly. She mentioned him unthinkingly a couple of times during the meal – how he had known the best New World dry whites to order, how he had been allergic to shellfish. Nick felt in contrast a pathetic failure – he had to admit when she asked that his previous relationship had ended not because his partner had had a terminal illness, but rather because she had buggered off to Barcelona and shacked up with a Catalan called Jordi. He sneezed again.

And then he asked about her job. "Oh, it's not as exciting as yours," she said, unknowingly scoring an own goal. She worked in insurance, for the Carlisle office of a specialist company which primarily insured farmers. "My dad and mum were farmers before they retired and my brother farms over near Brampton, so I guess it was sort of a natural thing to do," she said, with a nervous attempt at a laugh.

Nick found himself slipping into interviewer mode. "So, is insurance for farmers very different from what the rest of us get offered?" he asked.

Cheryl opened up. "Well, some of the products are much the same. But you've got to remember that agriculture is an occupation with high accident rates, so people want health cover, and income protection insurance, and life cover and so on. Then there's the risk of your barn burning down, and maybe taking all the previous season's crop or your livestock with it. There's all your farm equipment to insure. Quad bikes have been a particular favourite for thieves recently, and tractors too. Sometimes tractors will cost as much as a top of the range Mercedes, tens of thousands of pounds, and of course they often get left parked in isolated fields. Sheep rustling, would you believe it, we've had a recent rash of that, too..."

She paused, and then continued. "Anyway, that's what I do. Sorry, I'm probably boring you."

"Not at all," Nick responded.

The chicken and the fish had been finished and the plates cleared away. They looked at each other.

"Are we going to have puddings?" Nick asked.

"Do you know, I really don't think I want one," Cheryl replied.

They ordered coffee, talked a little more about nothing much, and split the bill 50-50 when it came. There was an unspoken acknowledgement by them both that they would not meet up again.

"Thank you, that was very pleasant," Cheryl said as they left.

"It was," Nick echoed.

He walked back to his car feeling more unhappy with his life that he had for a long time. Perhaps it was the cold he seemed to have picked up, which now was definitely getting worse. Perhaps it was the previous night catching up with him... or the fact that throughout the meal with Cheryl part of his brain had been working away, trying to make sense of how a simple news-story about a garden gate seemed to be turning out so strangely. He was also worried about the Rothburys. He didn't believe that anyone would ever show up to fix their gate, but someone had obviously felt it important enough to ring them up and to persuade them not to talk any more to him.

When he was back in the driving seat and had started the ignition he turned the car towards the M6, rather than the direct route back along the A595. The motorway was quiet and he quickly passed the Penrith and Shap turns, before deciding to pull in to the Tebay services. He grabbed a take-away coffee and got the mobile out. He had had a thought. He found the phone number for Penrith library through a web search and then put a call through. When they answered, he asked to be put through to the reference section.

From Tebay it was only about ten miles back into Kendal, back along the same road he'd taken the evening before. He skirted Kendal's town centre which was busy with Saturday afternoon shoppers and made his way through the network of suburban streets. He parked in a quiet side street in almost the same place he had found ten days or so earlier. The house he was aiming for still had its 'For Sale' sign in the garden.

Pauline Peters answered the door to his ring, but this time didn't invite him in. She obviously had someone round: behind her in the hall, Nick had a brief glimpse of another young woman, who rapidly disappeared from sight into the kitchen as the front door opened. Nick had a momentary thought that the woman's face seemed familiar, though he couldn't place it.

"Hello Pauline, it's Nick from the *Enquirer*," he said.

"I know," she said. She was standing with the front door half open, with her arms on her hips. It was not precisely a hostile gesture, but it certainly wasn't particularly welcoming.

"Sorry to turn up like this. It's just that I wanted some help. I wrote a story in last week's paper and inadvertently I may have put an elderly couple who live by themselves at some risk." He explained briefly the story as he had written it for the paper.

"I've no idea why you are telling me this," Pauline said when he finished.

Nick paused. "Because there may or may not be a connection with Davie," he said.

Pauline suddenly became tense.

"Yes?" she asked, a touch aggressively.

"I think Davie was probably the person driving the wagon. The person who gave his name as Rowan Atkinson." Nick went on to explain what he hadn't been able to publish in the paper.

"You did say that Davie sometimes borrowed your father's vehicle at weekends. If it was Davie, I don't need to know what he was doing. I just need you to tell me if you know of anyone he might have associated with. Someone maybe who is unhappy at what I've put in the paper. Someone who could take it out on the Rothburys."

Pauline said nothing for what seemed to Nick like a very long time. Eventually, she answered.

"I don't know what Davie did with the wagon."

"I believe you."

"I wouldn't tell you if I did know, but it's the honest truth that I don't know." She paused again. "But Davie wouldn't have ever done anything really bad. You must believe me on that too."

"OK," Nick replied neutrally.

There was silence again.

Pauline was still standing in the doorway, and was obviously waiting for Nick to say something more.

"Um, was there any reason why Davie might have wanted to – er – perhaps take a risk or two now and again? I mean, was he short of money?"

"Aren't we all these days?" Pauline replied brusquely.

The conversation was as difficult as it had been the first time Nick had door-stepped Pauline, before she had finally opened up to him. He persevered.

"Listen, have you got any information at all about who Davie might have had dealings with? A name?"

Pauline took even longer to reply. She appeared to be weighing up whether or not to trust Nick with an answer.

"There was someone called Marcus," she said eventually.

"Marcus?"

"That's really all I know. I don't know his surname or what he does. I heard Davie mention him a couple of times, but he never said anything more to me than that."

"OK, thank you, Pauline. How did Davie get in touch with Marcus?"

She shrugged. "No idea. Mobile phone probably."

"And would you have got a number for him? Have you by any chance got Davie's old phone, where the number might have been stored? Maybe you've found something when sorting out his flat?"

Pauline looked up, suddenly suspicious.

"How do you know I've been sorting out his flat?"

"Just a guess. Did you find anything?"

Again Pauline weighed up the answer. "OK, there was a bit of paper there in his handwriting, with the letter M and a mobile number below. It could mean anything or nothing."

"Have you got it?"

Pauline didn't reply, but made a move from the doorway back into her hall. "Don't come in," she added, over her shoulder. She returned a moment later, with a single piece of paper torn from a notebook.

"Here it is."

"Thank you," said Nick, writing down the number carefully.

"It's a wild goose chase. It probably wasn't Davie driving at all. You've got no proof."

"No, only circumstantial. Although there was one other strange thing I haven't mentioned." The act of writing down the mobile number had reminded Nick of the number that the lorry driver had proffered to Edgar Rothbury. Sally Smyth's number. At that moment, he had a mental image of the photo of Sally which he had found on her website. And at that moment he knew, too, without a shadow of a doubt, something else.

"The lorry driver had given Edgar Rothbury a phone number as his contact. It's Sally Smyth's number."

"What? I've no idea what you're talking about." Nick had forgotten that Pauline had chosen not to tell him about Sally when they'd met previously.

"I agree there's no obvious explanation," Nick said. And then he added: "Maybe I could ask Sally herself if she has any idea. I see that she's here visiting you."

Pauline looked at Nick aggressively. "It's time you took yourself away and stopped bothering me. I think I've already told you too much. Stupid me, I somehow thought I could trust you. I forgot that you can never trust anyone who works for the papers."

"You *can* trust me," Nick replied. But the conversation was clearly at an end. "Well, er, goodbye," he added. "And, please, tell Sally that I'm really sorry if she thought I was harassing her. I wasn't intending to." He turned to walk back to his car. Pauline shut the front door firmly as he went, saying nothing.

Nick turned up the car heating as he headed out of Kendal towards Windermere. He was conscious of his sore throat again, and desperate for another round of paracetamol tablets. Time to get home.

But as he approached the turn-off to Staveley, he changed his mind. It was late afternoon, and Lindsay would be just about to finish her shift at the café there. If she didn't have any paracetamol one of the other staff almost certainly would, and he could wash them down with a pot of tea. He eased the car through Staveley's narrow streets.

Lindsay was indeed just about to finish work. She brought a pot of tea, and the tablets, across to Nick and then came and joined him.

"So how did it go? What was she like?" Nick had mentioned the day before about the imminent rendezvous with Cheryl.

"She was nice, and I wasn't. I didn't make an effort. She deserved better." Nick sneezed.

"You got a cold?"

"Seems so. You know, Lindsay, I may stop this business with the lonely hearts ads. Somehow I almost can't be bothered any more. Perhaps I've lived by myself too long."

"You shouldn't be too hard on yourself. There'll be someone out there who's right for you."

"Maybe. But I want to talk to you about something else."

"I do too. Davie."

Nick nodded, and drank from the mug of tea.

Lindsay went on. "How well did we know him? I mean, we knew he was a fantastic runner, but what else did we really know?" She paused. "We didn't even know about Sally the sculptor."

"No, you're right. And if it was Davie driving the wagon, what precisely was he doing?"

"I've no idea. I thought it might be drugs. Perhaps Under Cragg farm is used to grow dope plants. There's a lot of that happening at the moment. It's a long way off the beaten track, and the two chained-up dogs would put off casual visitors."

"If it was drugs, why would you need Davie's wagon? A white van would be rather more discreet."

Nick had another gulp of tea. "By the way, I phoned up the library earlier today to find out who's on the electoral roll at Under Cragg. There's just one man registered there, a man with the name of William Shutter. Oh, and there's a couple called Michael and Amanda Sutcliffe at the other farm, the one which was in darkness last night. I asked for their names too whilst I was at it."

"OK, William Shutter." Lindsay was mulling over this information. "If it's not drugs what else could Mr Shutter be doing?"

"The only conceivable idea I have had up to now is that there could be some scam going on with illegal immigrants," Nick replied. There was a moment's silence: Nick knew that Lindsay was thinking of the terrible event in Morecambe Bay in 2004 when twenty-one Chinese migrant workers had lost their lives, drowned by the incoming tide whilst picking cockles. Even in quiet country areas of England remote from the big cities, there were people forced to suffer lives of scarcely imaginable exploitation. Living among us, but living apart from us.

"I really hope you're wrong," Lindsay said. "That doesn't sound like Davie to me."

There was a silence between them.

"I've found out something else, too," said Nick. He briefly summarised his conversation with Pauline about the man called Marcus. Lindsay grimaced.

"Better take care, Nick. Don't do anything stupid."

"I won't. But it's made me think again about the Bowfell race. What do you think happened at the Bad Step?"

"Did Davie lose his footing, or...?" She stopped.

"That's the question I'm asking myself. What's the answer?"

"I've no idea. I suppose someone could have been out to get Davie. Maybe he'd got himself mixed up in some nasty stuff. Anyone who knew Davie would have known what he was doing that afternoon, and the weather would have provided pretty good cover."

"Yes, and they'd have known that Davie was likely to be one of the first runners to arrive at the Bad Step. Still, they would have had to go to a lot of trouble. Climbed up to the Crinkle Crags for a start. Why do all that?"

"To make it seem just like an accident? People get injured and die in accidents in the Cumbrian mountains all the time. The mountain rescue teams are always having to turn out to deal with incidents like that," Lindsay said.

"I still prefer to think that Davie just slipped. It's a horrible thought otherwise," Nick responded.

They were silent again.

"Well, let's wait and see if anyone else chooses to ring the paper to report on broken garden gates," Nick said, eventually.

"Actually, there's something I can do when I get to work. That area around Under Cragg is outside my local authority patch, it's Eden council's responsibility, but I know one of the planners who works for them. If you like, I'll ring him. He'll know if there's been any unusual planning applications down that way recently."

"OK," Nick said, and sneezed.

"Time you got home to bed," Lindsay said. She gave him a peck on the cheek, and turned back to the kitchen.

In the end, Nick decided to make one other short stop on the journey home. Generally, he tried when he could to support the small independent cooperative shops which you could still find in Cumbrian villages like Coniston and Chapel Stile, where the villagers were the coop members and the profits ended up back in the community. But sometimes he needed things urgently. He turned into the carpark of the large supermarket just by Windermere station and rushed in.

The supermarket was half-empty. The day visitors had left the Lake District and most locals were back home, getting ready for the Saturday evening meal. Nick picked up a basket, put in two packets of paracetamol and then made for the alcohol section. He normally didn't drink whisky, but a medicinal hot toddy seemed today like a particularly good idea.

"Well, dear boy, that doesn't look so very appetising." There was someone else in the drinks aisle who was addressing him.

Nick looked up. "Hello, George," he said. The other shopper was George Mulholland. Nick looked down at his basket and suddenly realised that the two packets of pain-killers and the half bottle of scotch, all he had so far put in the basket, could be open to misinterpretation. Especially to a policeman used to dealing with the less happy side of human existence.

"Life treating you all right I hope?" George said.

"Lousy cold, but otherwise fine."

George Mulholland's own basket was hardly much fuller, the main item in it being a cardboard tube which clearly contained a bottle of malt whisky.

"A bottle of Islay's finest," George said in response to the unasked question from Nick. "Islay malt is what the French would call my péché mignon, my little sin. This one's from the distillery with the most beautiful location in Scotland, on Islay's coast right beside the Sound of Jura. You can look across the water to the mountains of Jura beyond."

"The Paps of Jura. There's a famous fell race over them once a year." Nick took advantage of the cue he had been offered. "Talking of such things, have you any more news of how the coroner is progressing with Davie Peters? It's been exactly two weeks since it happened."

"Ah yes, the unfortunate young Mr Peters. Well, coroners like to do things in their own good time. But I suspect he'll at least be able to release the body soon for the funeral."

"Any more talk of an inquest?"

"Not clear yet, old boy. If there is to be an inquest, the coroner will open it formally and then immediately adjourn it, I expect. It can take months to get all the evidence together, but of course you're a journalist, you'll know all this." Nick didn't, but told himself that he should have known it.

"I gather that you've been down to Leeds to interview Steve Miller, the runner who won that day," Nick said. He was interested to see how the detective inspector would respond.

"Ah now, yes, I do believe you may be right. It's important to leave no stone unturned, I always say to each new intake of DCs. Of course Mr Miller would be a witness if there were to be an inquest. The race marshals too, and the organiser."

George Mulholland turned the conversation. "But tell me, what are the big scoops you're chasing? My life these days is a sad one, filling in so much paperwork that I need someone like you to say what's happening in the outside world."

Nick laughed. "The usual things. Nothing very exciting." He took a split-second decision. "Though there's an elderly couple living out by themselves beyond Kendal whom you and your colleagues might want to keep half an eye on. I wrote an article in this week's paper about a lorry driver who damaged their garden gate last week, and it sounds as if they have had a threatening phone call since the paper came out. Don't quite know why a large wagon was in such a small lane."

"It's a sad world when older folk can't enjoy their retirement in peace, is it not?" George appeared not particularly interested in what Nick had said. "Now, next time we have a drink together, I will initiate you into the liquid amber delights of the island of Islay," he went on. Nick noticed that he had been eyeing up with considerable disdain the half-bottle in Nick's basket, a mass-market blend. "I can see, dear boy, that your education needs to be taken firmly in hand."

Chapter 15

Cheryl was rushing to complete the claims paperwork for a burglary one of their clients had suffered at his farm near the Solway Firth when the phone on her desk rang. It was Mary on the switchboard. Someone wanted specifically to talk to her, Mary said. Cheryl sighed, as she heard the call being put through.

"Hello?"

"Cheryl, it's – er – Nick here."

"Nick! I'm surprised to hear from you. You're ringing me at work, you know."

"I know I am. And I'm sorry, but this is a work type of call I'm making."

"Yes?"

"There was something you mentioned on Saturday which I wanted to ask you about."

Nick had spent almost all of Sunday in bed. Saturday's hot toddy had failed to work its magic. There could be no doubt now that he had a really bad Autumn cold.

He'd tried to read some of the background material for his book, but had very quickly given up. Then he'd read a few pages of a light novel he'd picked up a few weeks back in the local Oxfam shop, though that too failed to hold his attention. He switched on Radio 4, which was in the middle of the Archers Sunday omnibus, moved across to Radio 3 which was deep in some concert of baroque music, and then retuned again to Radio 5 Live. He paid no attention to the programme, but the sound of people murmuring away in the background was somehow reassuring.

Then he'd slept. And then he had woken again, with an interesting idea in his head. It would, however, mean a phone call to Cheryl as soon as he was back at work. He hoped she wouldn't misunderstand.

He had found the phone number of her office without difficulty in the directory, and had persuaded the woman on the switchboard to put him through. "When you were talking to me about your work," he went on, "you mentioned that among other things you'd had some claims for sheep rustling recently. I was wondering how many? And whereabouts?"

"Is that why you're ringing me?"

"Well, yes. I'm afraid I'm being a journalist at the moment."

There was silence as Cheryl considered this. "I'm not sure what I can tell you," she said. "All the claims are confidential, and anyway we're not authorised to talk to the media. I suppose you could ring our head office."

"Right…" It was Nick's turn to consider. "I understand. Is there anyone else locally you know I could talk about this to?"

"Well, Peter Gaukroger is the regional National Farmers Union rep, he might be able to help you. Then there's PC Mick Masters over in Penrith, he's the wildlife and animal crime policeman for much of the Lakes. Do you want their numbers?"

Nick wrote them down.

"Thank you, Cheryl." It was time to end the call, and he wasn't quite sure what to say next.

"I'm sorry if Saturday wasn't quite what it could have been. My fault, I think," he eventually said.

"Don't apologise, it was nice to have your company." And then, with a genuine note of concern in her voice, "How is your cold today? I hope you're feeling better."

"I am, thank you Cheryl," Nick replied. The call ended.

In fact, he was not feeling better, but he had dragged himself to work. Molly seemed unaware of his condition, and had in fact begun the day with what could almost have counted as a bollocking.

"Nick, you really must get that fell-runner story finished off, you know. You seem to be spending inordinate amounts of time of it. I can't give you much longer," she'd told him.

"Pretty well finished, but I'm just waiting for the coroner to pronounce," Nick had responded, disingenuously. He knew very well it was nowhere near finished.

He rang Peter Gaukroger of the NFU, but the answerphone message told Nick that he was on leave. PC Masters was working, however, and was more than happy to talk.

"It's a big problem at the moment," the policeman had said in answer to Nick's question. "It's the price of lamb, you see. It's almost doubled in the past few months. A good quality Texel ewe could go for as much as £80 or £90 at auction, so imagine it: a field miles from anywhere with the equivalent of little stacks of £20 notes all grazing away, ready to be picked up. We've got gangs of criminals in the Lakes at the moment doing just that."

"How many sheep get taken?"

"It varies, but we had 100 taken a few weeks back not far from Maryport, and about eighty went from a field north of Penrith. A year or two back we had about twenty cases of rustling a year, but now it's becoming almost an epidemic."

"Easy pickings, I guess."

"Yes, but not that easy. You need to know what you're doing. Basically, you need to have someone involved who's experienced in livestock handling, and maybe a sheepdog as well. Plus a wagon or trailer to take the sheep away in, of course."

The policeman paused and then went on.

"Farmers hate the idea of rustling not only because they're losing valuable stock but also because of who commits the crime. It often turns out to be people who are local, perhaps with a background in farming. People who know when farmers will out in their fields and when they won't be."

"When would rustling generally go on? At weekends, say? Sundays?"

"Weekends? Well, that's always possible although the usual time is at night or during the week when a big livestock auction is going on in one of the towns. That's when many farmers will be away from their farms."

"And what happens to the sheep?"

"Butchered in a back-street establishment and sold on the black market to the food trade, I expect."

"Have you had any recent cases down in the south-east of Cumbria?" Nick asked, trying to keep the note of eagerness from his voice. He mentioned the names of the two or three villages nearest to Under Cragg Farm. He was quietly confident that his hunch was going to prove correct.

But Mick Masters didn't give the reply Nick had expected. "No, nothing at all down there, I'm pleased to say."

"Would you get to hear if sheep rustling had happened thereabouts? Say, over the past few weeks?"

"Oh yes, I think so, normally I'd be the first to know. All crime like that in Cumbria should get reported to me," the policeman responded.

Nick thanked him for his help and rang off, just as Molly came across to his desk.

"So what have you got for me if the fell-runner piece isn't available?" She still sounded impatient with him.

"Sheep rustling, I hope. I'm in the middle of making some calls," he replied. He should at least be able to offer a story of some kind to satisfy Molly – PC Masters had given him some adequate quotes on the phone – but just how big a story it would be would depend on the next call of the day which needed to be made. This would be to a mobile phone number he had been given on Saturday afternoon. The one associated with the letter 'M'.

Nick had pondered this call carefully. He didn't want to make the mistakes he'd made in trying to ring Sally Smyth, and he suspected that he'd only get one chance to get what he needed, which was confirmation of exactly what had been going on down by Under Cragg. He also felt that M, if M was who he expected him to be, would not pick up a call where the caller's number was withheld. On the other hand, he didn't want to ring from a number which could be easily traced to the *Enquirer*, or from his own personal mobile. Better take care, Lindsay had told him when they'd talked on Saturday.

He'd come up with a solution, although it had cost him £30. He'd called in on his way to work and bought the cheapest pay-as-you-go mobile package from one of the mobile phone shops in Windermere. So he now had a phone, and he now had a phone number, which he intended to reserve just for this one call – and for any subsequent incoming calls which might come back to him as a consequence.

His morning purchases had been completed with a bag of cough sweets from a Windermere chemist. He didn't particularly want his voice to be too recognisable. It was a problem that he still had a London accent although, fortunately, he was sounding distinctly more croaky than usual. However, he decided that he'd also pop one of the sweets in his mouth when he made the call. That should do the trick.

"Just going outside for a few minutes," he told Molly, who was peering at her screen, typing away furiously. He felt surprisingly nervous. Pull yourself together, you're supposed to be a professional at this sort of thing, he told himself.

He punched M's number into his new mobile and waited. The ringing sound from the other end carried on and on and Nick was about to ring off when, abruptly, the call was answered.

"Yes?" said a voice.

"Is that Marcus?" asked Nick, sucking furiously at the sweet.

"It could be. Who's ringing?" came the reply. Nick had somehow expected that Marcus would have a polished public school voice, but what he heard at the other end of the phone was a local accent. What Nick also heard in the voice, however, was a great deal of self-confidence.

"I'm Pete. You don't know me, but I'm an old school friend of Davie Peters. Davie told me what he was doing for you, and – well, I know it's terrible about the accident he had – but the fact is, I was wondering whether you were looking for someone to take over. You know, do the driving."

There was a silence at the other end, as this information was absorbed.

"Do you have a wagon?" the voice asked him.

"Yes. At weekends, like Davie had. I wouldn't have rung you otherwise."

"So, Pete, tell me more about yourself. What else do you do?"

"Well, I do some driving work for other people, you know, casual like." Nick sucked again at the sweet. "Otherwise, nothing much."

"All right," came the reply. And then, abruptly: "There's something funny about your voice."

"Sorry, Marcus, I'm chewing something. Gum."

"Hmm. So, have you got the experience I'd need?"

"Oh yes, as I said, I've got my driving licence for the wagon." This was going better than Nick had hoped. It was going too well. "And I've plenty of experience with livestock."

There was silence. "What did you just say?"

Nick faltered. "I can help handling the livestock," he said.

The silence returned. Then the voice spoke sharply to him. "Listen, son, you've got the wrong number." Another pause. "I suggest you forget that you made this call."

The line went dead.

Nick returned indoors, feeling exhausted. The sudden transition into the heated office, filled with Molly's cigarette smoke, started a sneezing fit. God, he wasn't feeling at all good. Not that Molly had yet noticed. She came across, as he regained his chair, and spoke to him.

"Sheep rustling's a good idea, assuming you can stand the story up. Can you get it finished by first thing tomorrow?"

Nick hadn't the energy to tell her that, far from standing up, his story appeared suddenly to be lying on its back, waving its legs ineffectually in the air. He muttered a reply: "Will do my best."

It's the nature of work that everyone has difficult days. But by four o'clock Nick had definitely had enough. Coughing and sneezing, he made his way out to his car. A quiet evening in, a little bit of mindless television watching and then an early bed, complete with hot water bottle and another hot toddy – that was what, he decided, he needed.

A quiet evening.

Sometime just before six, as Nick was over in the kitchen beginning to start the work of scrambling some eggs, he was conscious that it had suddenly appeared to have gone dark. Admittedly the nights were drawing in now, but there should have been at least another half-hour of daylight to enjoy. Perhaps there was a serious storm on its way across the mountains.

He came through to the living room, and realised to his surprise that something was blocking out almost all the light from the front window. What could be a very large coach appeared to have driven up his road and parked immediately outside. At that moment, a hammering began at the front door. Nick went across to open it.

It was a lorry, not a coach, parked outside and its driver was on the doorstep.

"You little shit."

The man had already started shouting at him.

"You're a filthy piece of shit. You think you're the bee's knees with your fancy London ways but people like you, you're scum."

The man was middle-aged, about six foot tall, and very very angry.

"My dog craps turds that are worth more than you. How dare you meddle in my affairs? Mr-bleeding-reporter, sticking his bloody nose into everything. Well, you can bloody well get your nose out again and leave me and my family in peace. Do I make myself clear?"

Nick had taken some moments to work out who his visitor could be.

"Mr Peters?" he asked.

"Oh, it's *Mr* Peters, it's always *Mr* Peters. Oh yes, pretend to be all polite, it's all a clever game for people like you, isn't it. And you never think of the consequences of what you do. Have you...." The voice grew louder. "Have you ever thought what it's like to lose one of your children? No, of course you haven't, all you want is your lousy little news story."

"No, really..."

"Do you know what my family have had to go through in the past two weeks? The coroner who won't give us the body, can you understand that? And the visits to my wife from fucking Paddy Richards, standing on the doorstep day after day with his black briefcase and speaking loudly just to make sure all our neighbours can hear him."

"I'm sorry, but I honestly don't know..." Nick got no further.

"I thought Richards was an arsehole, but you're worse. At least Richards is honest about his job. You don't even know the meaning of the word. Honestly? Don't make me laugh. I suppose you'll pretend that you haven't been talking to the police. Oh I expect you thought, what *Mr* Peters really wants is a visit from the boys in blue to cheer him up. Except it wasn't the boys in blue, was it, it was that reptile Mulholland. He's always had it in for me. One small mistake several years ago, people like Mulholland never forget."

"You had a visit from...?"

"Just a few short questions, Mr Peters, if I might. That's what he said. And then the bloody interrogation starts. What have you been using your wagon for, Mr Peters? What did Davie use the wagon for? Would it be too much trouble, Mr Peters, if I were to have a look inside the wagon? Oh, no, of course not, Mr Mulholland, absolutely no bleeding trouble at all. Make yourself at home."

There was a slight pause, before he continued.

"Who got the police involved, eh? It must have been you."

"No, really, you're making a mistake…"

"A mistake? I don't think so. Pauline told me you'd been round to her place on Saturday, wheedling your way into her confidence. I bet you rushed away and immediately chatted to your mate Mulholland. You and he, you're two of a kind. Go on, deny it if you can."

Nick thought back to Saturday afternoon.

"Er, well I did see Mulholland in the supermarket later on, but I really didn't say anything to him…"

"You admit it, I knew it. I'd like to smash your face into pulp but, you know what, I'm not going to bother. Because you're not worth it. You're a heap of slime already. But just remember this, *Mr* Potterton, I never want to hear of you again. Fuck off out of my life."

He turned away, without waiting for a reply. Nick closed the front door, and heard the diesel engine of the lorry start. With loud revving, it disappeared from sight down the road.

Chapter 16

He generally described himself as a businessman. Well yes, a successful businessman.

And sometimes, when for example he and Chantelle were enjoying drinks with their English neighbours out on the terrace by the pool on the new development outside Marbella where he had bought the holiday villa a few years back, cradling their glasses and looking down as the sun shone warm and red high over the Mediterranean below them, he would accept the term entrepreneur. To be an entrepreneur involved taking risk, and he had taken plenty of risks in building up the business, putting his own money on the line.

If you asked further, he would tell you that he was in the finance business. That as a rule was as much as most people wanted to know.

But just occasionally, let's say when the wine had flowed and the paella pan had been picked clean of the last few mussels and clams and pieces of chicken and he and Chantelle and a handful of particular friends remained behind to watch as the sky darkened first to velvet blue and then into blue-black night, he would tell you that, really, if you thought about it, what he did was to provide a valuable social service. Really the government ought to recognise what he did and give him a tax break. And everyone would laugh.

No, listen to me, he'd say. We live in a world where credit is an essential feature of daily life, just as necessary as drinking water out of the tap or electricity out of the socket. And if for some reason or other you are deemed by large institutions over which you have absolutely no control not to be worthy of credit, you are effectively excluded from being able to play your part in normal life. Forced to play by harsher, stricter rules than everybody else around you. Marginalised.

Of course, the banks and the building societies couldn't care less. God knows they make enough money, but they make it by taking as few risks as they possibly can, by refusing to lend to you if they feel that in any way you aren't a rock-solid cast-iron proposition, if let's say your credit score is slightly down because maybe you have moved around a fair bit in your life or you don't own your own house or you don't have an old-fashioned nine-to-five job with an employment contract and all that kind of thing.

The banks don't need to worry about those they turn away from their doors. If, let's say, you need a small advance to tide you over just for a few weeks so you can buy the kids' Christmas presents or pay off the gas bill they couldn't give a damn. Or a flying fuck.

Whereas, whenever he could, he was prepared to help. If you came to him and said, Paddy, what about it, what's the chance of a couple of hundred pounds just until the end of the month, nine times out of ten he'd pull out the notes there and then, ten crisp twenty pound notes, and hand them to you. Of course, there'd be a little paperwork to complete, but generally he tried to keep things as simple as possible for his clients. Clients, that was the word he preferred. Why did everyone these days insist on always talking about 'customers'?

The basic deal was easy to understand. You'd borrow, let's say, that £200 you needed and you'd pay it back in a month's time, together with a bit of interest. The interest was 10% a month, so it was easy to calculate: you'd pay back £220, and you'd be quits. Or he'd lend you £500 and you'd give him back £550. What could be more straight-forward than that?

Of course, he said, there were always some people around, people like politicians or journalists with particular axes to grind, who every so often would complain about his line of business. They'd claim that these sorts of interest rates were exorbitant and that the poorest people in society were being fleeced. He took little notice. He knew from experience that after a few weeks, or more likely a few days, they'd find something else to complain about and move on. Only very occasionally in the twelve years he'd been running his business had he had to put things on hold for a couple of weeks. Before getting back to normal again.

If you thought about it, it was obvious that his interest rate would have to be more than what a bank would charge. Firstly, the banks had first pick at lending to all those nice low-risk people with regular jobs and steady wages. He was prepared to take on those people they'd turned down. What's more, there was also much more work for him than for a bank in arranging the loans and getting the money back. He actually offered his clients the convenience of a doorstep service, and of course there were business costs associated with this. He had to factor in the time involved in trailing round all of Cumbria and parts of Lancashire and Weardale too. Not that he did this routine collection work any more, that was why he employed Barry and Gaz, of course.

There were other business expenses which he had to meet. The Land Rover Discovery, for example, which he kept solely for business use. Evenings and at weekends, when he and Chantelle went away for a break somewhere romantic, say, the Discovery would be safely parked in the garage and it would be the Beamer that he would be driving. Chantelle had her little soft-top of course, for her own use. But the Discovery was necessary: somehow his clients expected him to arrive in a vehicle like that.

He liked to dress well. No doubt he could have afforded to spend more, but he had long tended to favour suits from Paul Smith, partly because he liked the way they were cut. He worked out once a week in a private gym close to home to keep fit, and he found that the tailoring flattered the shape of his body well. His current favourite was a rather nice three-piece suit with a paisley print lining which he had bought in Manchester in the summer and which had come in at just under £1000. At the same time he'd also chosen a lovely pale green camel-wool coat ready for the colder Autumn days. That had been a little more, but worth every penny. Shoes, too – you really couldn't skimp when it came to footwear.

In any case clients expected him well-dressed, in the same way as people wanted their banks to be grand buildings with fancy stonework and great big wooden doors. It reassured them that you were solid, reliable, dependable.

So he had to make sure that his business brought in the income that was needed to meet all these outgoings, not to mention Chantelle's wardrobe and the prep school fees for the two lads. And there was more: if you were lending money, you had to factor in the risk that people would default. Banks allowed for this in the interest they charged, of course, and he did the same.

In practice, though, defaults weren't really a problem. Just as banks had their own credit enforcement teams who would ring up and hound their customers if they were late on a credit card payment he had his own arrangements in place, though he preferred to use the term credit control for this side of things. In really difficult cases, he would outsource the problem to big Jim who had his own ways of trying to explain to clients the serious situation they were in. Jim tended to be pretty successful at getting the message across, and most times the clients would once again start their payments, all sweetness and light. But actually if he had to call in Jim he was in a sense having to admit defeat.

He was careful to explain to his clients the arrangements when he first offered to help them, so that there could be no misunderstandings later. What happened if, for whatever reason, you found that you couldn't repay the money and the interest at the end of the month was that the late payment penalty charge cut in. Again, he liked to keep things simple. Basically, the interest rate was doubled. This was how it carried on until the amount you'd borrowed and the interest which had accumulated was paid off in full.

Because, human nature being what it is, most people found it necessary to miss a payment at least every so often, it did mean that interest rates generally were rather more than the basic 10%. He had quite a number of his clients who were now paying over 100% a month, and even some where the late payment charges had meant that the interest had gone up to over 300% a month. All the details were carefully recorded in the loan books which Barry and Gaz took around with them, and on his main business computer database back at the office at home.

If you totted up the totals outstanding on all the loans he had made, you would have concluded that he was quite astonishingly wealthy. But actually that wasn't relevant. He knew for a certain fact that he would never see all this notional money he was owed. Rather, his business demonstrated the old maxim that the secret of a successful business operation is a healthy cash flow. The key was in making sure that the monthly payments were coming in from the clients in a nice steady stream, and that little by little these monthly payments were increasing. The real success of his business was the client base he had built up over the previous twelve years. With very few exceptions, once a client, always a client.

The relationship with them was important. He prided himself on this aspect of his business, he wanted them to feel that he was approachable. He encouraged them to call him Paddy. Actually, the name in his passport was Phillip Richards, but Paddy, he thought, had a nice familiar feel to it. Sometimes, too, it could help if both clients and the authorities were slightly confused on this point. When it came to work, he was Paddy.

In every well-functioning system, however, there are always a few people who manage to put a spoke in the wheels. And, no doubt about it, Davie Peters fell into that category.

Frankly, he'd probably been wrong to take Davie on. Davie wasn't really one of his typical clients. Mostly he got new clients by word of mouth. They tended to be families who had unexpectedly fallen on difficult times – an illness, perhaps, or a redundancy which had come out of the blue – or single parents bringing up young kids and finding that their state benefits were just not enough for the everyday costs of life, or people whose marriages had gone belly up, or sometimes pensioner couples who were struggling to get by on the state pension and failing. People who had somehow failed to manage to play the rules of the game successfully. The newspapers probably would lump them all together as benefits scroungers.

But Davie hadn't been like that. Had things been different, Paddy could have even seen Davie working for him in his business rather than as a client. He recognised him as something of a kindred spirit. He understood Davie's drive to succeed and the risks he was prepared to run to get what he wanted.

They'd met for the first time late one Friday afternoon in a pub in Kendal, two or three years back when Davie had still had his job with the local council. Davie had been having a drink or two with some of his mates from work, and spending a little of the wages that had come his way. They were playing pontoon, for low stakes. He'd come over, and been persuaded to join in.

After an hour or so, Davie had turned down the offer of the drink one of the others had made and had got up to leave. The cards must have treated Davie badly that day – he'd lost perhaps twenty pounds – and he was obviously getting to the point where he knew he wouldn't have enough cash later on to buy his own round back. Paddy had stepped in. Somehow or other by the end of the afternoon Davie had an extra £50 in his pocket and Paddy had a new client.

It wasn't the usual way these things started and from the beginning Paddy, professionally speaking, had had an uncomfortable feeling that there might be problems ahead. In fact, Davie's debt towards him rose remarkably quickly so that after less than nine months it had crossed into four figures. The repayments were coming in, after a fashion, though the penalty interest rate was climbing steadily too. The real problem for Paddy, though, was why Davie wanted the money.

Most people borrowed to cope with their household expenses, or to put food on the table for the kids, or to keep up with the rent or the mortgage payments. Davie wasn't in this category. He was borrowing money because he thought he could use it to make more money, and it made him very reckless. Paddy wasn't sure that he liked having clients who were quite so reckless.

Gaz would normally have covered collections in the Ambleside area but unusually Paddy had told him that he would deal with Davie himself. It meant that he could keep a close watch on Davie's account. He'd finally told Davie earlier in the summer that he'd stop making any further advances, but the problem from then on was that Davie in exchange had immediately stopped any pretence of making repayments. Paddy had already had to have a quiet discussion about the way forward with Jim, but he wasn't sure that even Jim would get results. What Paddy knew, but didn't know whether Davie knew, is that ultimately Davie could call Paddy's bluff. Just not pay.

And then, after all this, somehow it had happened that Davie had fallen down a mountain and come a cropper big time. Whoops!

This was new territory for Paddy. But each new challenge brings an opportunity, as they say, and he hadn't become a successful businessman by chance.

He turned the Discovery round the corner into the road where Davie's parents lived. He was getting to know the way pretty well. He'd been round three times already, each time taking care to check that the father's wagon wasn't parked beside the house so that he would be able to get Davie's mother by herself. So far she'd managed to send him away empty-handed, but Paddy had a shrewd idea that he was successfully wearing her down. He was quietly confident that this time he'd get what he needed from her – the signature.

His standard borrowing form included a section where the client had to fill in the name and address of their next of kin. It meant that Paddy had the names both of Davie's parents and of the place where they lived. Of course, if you wanted to be *technical* about things, if you were determined to insist on the letter of the law, then it could well be that you might want to argue that this part of the form was rather superfluous – that actually Paddy had no right in assuming that your relatives would feel that they had any sort of responsibility in taking over the repayments on the borrowings which you yourself had made, should the eventuality arise that you had, very unfortunately, passed away. But in the few previous cases where Paddy had had to invoke this clause, he found that generally people didn't make this argument.

His case was, he felt, persuasive. Surely, he would say of the dead person to the grieving relatives, you're not thinking of *excluding* them, of claiming that they weren't part of your family. Surely you wouldn't want people to think that you don't acknowledge them in this way.

And whilst the signature which, in the end, they put on the pieces of paper which Paddy proffered them might, again technically speaking, not necessarily be watertight in a court of law, who was talking anyway of the law? The signature seemed to do the trick. It seemed to be enough to ensure that the regular monthly payments continued to come in, that Paddy's cash flow stayed as buoyant as ever.

Margaret Peters had initially been shocked, and then angry, when he had first approached her. She was clearly astonished at the size of the borrowings her son had run up. But Paddy had given her time to get used to this. He was sure, he told himself as he pushed the bell and waited for her to open the front door, that this trip would see her bow to the inevitable. Fourth time lucky.

And, indeed, it was.

Chapter 17

"Nick?" It was Lindsay ringing his mobile number.

"Hi Lindsay."

"How's the cold?"

"Better, I think. Though I had to frighten it away with a massive hot toddy last night. My liver may never forgive me."

After Gary Peters' visit on Monday evening, Nick had reached for the whisky before crawling away upstairs and almost immediately falling asleep. Whether it was the drink or whether it was the sleep he wasn't sure, but something seemed to have helped. He woke up on Tuesday feeling that he could face the new day. Well, it surely couldn't be worse than the day before.

Molly had greeted him when he got in to work with a welcoming wave from across the office. She seemed to have left Monday's grumpiness behind and her mood matched the turquoise fisherman's smock affair which she had chosen to put on. The slacks underneath were a cheerful shade of bright yellow.

"Morning, Nick," she'd said brightly.

"Anything I need to know?"

"There's a press conference on Friday morning over at Grizedale Forest Park I wanted to talk to you about. New facilities for mountain bikers or something. I told them I'd go, but I was wondering if you would cover it instead. I know it's a Friday, which isn't normally your day, but I could give you some time in lieu next week."

Nick thought quickly. With Rosa coming at the weekend, it would make sense to defer spending time on his book until after she'd been. "That should be OK, I think."

"Our outdoor correspondent. I think they're going to give you a chance to have a spin on their bikes," Molly said.

Nick moved across to his desk. He had barely had a chance to turn on his computer before Lindsay had rung through. She had some news of her own.

"What are you doing at lunchtime?" she asked. "I've heard back from the planner I know, the guy I rang up about Under Cragg. He says he thinks he's got something to show you which he thinks you'll find interesting. He sounded very excited, but he refused to say anything more on the phone. He suggested meeting us both over a sandwich."

"An early lunch would be fine. 12.30pm?"

"Fine, I'll ring him back and arrange it. His name's Paul Ryburne, by the way."

They met Paul in a café close to Lindsay's office in Kendal. He was in a grey suit which looked as if it had seen better days, and had a large briefcase with him which he put down on the table. He wore round-rimmed glasses which gave him a rather owlish expression. Almost everything about his appearance said local government.

"Hello," he said. "You must be Nick Potterton."

"I am," Nick replied. "Lindsay said you had something to show me."

Paul said nothing, but reached into his briefcase and pulled out two large aerial photographs which he passed carefully to Nick.

"These are interesting, I think," he said at last.

Lindsay leaned across and she and Nick both looked at the photographs Paul had provided.

"They are photos of an area of limestone pavement," Nick said.

"Exactly," Paul responded.

"This looks like where we went last week. That's Under Cragg, isn't it?" Lindsay chipped in, pointing towards a small group of buildings roughly in the centre of the photo.

"Yes – oh, and that looks like the Rothbury's bungalow down there in the corner," Nick added.

"Yes," Paul said.

"The two photos are identical," Nick said after studying them for a moment.

"Ah, no, that's where you're wrong," Paul replied. "Look more closely."

Nick and Lindsay peered again at the photos. It didn't help that they'd chosen a quiet table, well away from other customers but also well away from the main overhead light in the room.

"This first photo is one we happened to have on file from 2007. And this one… " Paul picked it up as he spoke "…is a new one, one I ordered through yesterday after you'd rung me, Lindsay. There is one significant difference. Look again."

"Ah, maybe I've got it. Just above Under Cragg the land looks a bit different. Is that what you mean?" Nick asked.

"Precisely," Paul said triumphantly.

"Sorry, but I can't immediately see why this is significant," Nick said.

"Well, it should be pretty obvious, I'd have thought. Here we are in 2007, with a nice bit of limestone pavement just next to Under Cragg," Paul said, holding one of the photos. "And now turn the clock forward. Here we are today, with *no* nice bit of limestone pavement," he carried on, waving the other photo.

"So the limestone has gone?"

"It *has!*" Paul was jubilant. "Proof positive!"

"Somebody has moved it?" Lindsay said, questioningly.

"Somebody has indeed moved it," Paul replied. "Let us, for the sake of argument, proceed on the hypothesis that someone local, perhaps the local farmer, has chosen to remove it with a digger. And that someone else, someone equipped with a suitable lorry, has then driven along and removed the rocks."

There was a moment of silence as Nick and Lindsay absorbed this information. It was broken by a great guffaw from Nick.

"Rocks! I can't believe it. What you're suggesting is that Davie, if it was Davie, was simply carting away some rocks. Bloody hell, and I had convinced myself that he was up to something dodgy. I'd thought he was breaking the law! God, I can't tell you how relieved I am to hear that," he said.

It was Paul's turn to looked stunned.

"But, no, don't you understand?" he said. "What he was doing was most definitely breaking the law. That's what I have been trying to tell you."

"Right," Nick said, after a moment's pause. "Start at the beginning."

Chapter 18

Nick ended up working late that day. The lights were on in the office, blazing out into the dark night outside. Even Molly, who worked prodigiously long hours as a matter of course, had left an hour or so back. She'd turned off her monitor, put on her coat, and told Nick not to carry on too long.

He was focused on the story he had been working on for most of the afternoon and which was beginning to take shape on the screen in front of him. At this moment, he was particularly trying to nail down the opening paragraph. Generally speaking, if you could get the opening of a story right the rest of it fell into place relatively easily.

He had two possible openings which he was playing around with. One began as follows:

> Callous criminals are targeting one of Cumbria's most
> distinctive and beautiful landscapes. Evidence from aerial
> photographs seen by the *Enquirer* points to the illegal
> destruction of limestone pavement in parts of the county.

This was OK, but perhaps a little dry. The alternative went like this:

> Thoughtless gardeners are putting one of England's most
> beautiful landscapes at risk. Demand for water-worn rockery
> stone, often described as Westmorland Stone or Cumberland
> Stone, is behind the trade in illegally quarried limestone
> pavement, a unique and protected habitat. New evidence
> emerged this week of continuing removal of pavement in parts
> of Cumbria.

This had the benefit of linking the story with the readers themselves, or at least with those of them who were keen gardeners. Nick was veering towards this version.

Initially he hadn't taken what Paul Ryburne had told him very seriously. It seemed like just another petty planning rule, of the sort local government officers seemed to relish. Paul himself came over as pleasant enough, good at his job no doubt, but also a little plodding and worthy. Nick had found himself switching into hostile interviewing mode.

"It may technically be against the law, but it's hard to understand what the fuss is about taking away a few bits of boulder and rock," he'd said, between mouthfuls of the Mediterranean vegetable ciabatta he had ordered.

"Not just any old bits of boulder, though," Paul had replied patiently. "Lindsay told me you visited the limestone pavement areas yourselves a week or so back. You must have got a sense of how special the landscape is."

"True," Nick had been forced to respond. "It's just that there's an obsession these days with making regulations about everything. Maybe so that people like you can keep your jobs."

Paul had not taken the bait. Instead, he had persevered, talking to Nick quietly and slowly in the sort of way in which you might try to pass on your professional expertise to a group of slightly dim trainees.

And he was thorough. In the end, he and Nick had carried on talking in the café for the best part of an hour, staying on well after Lindsay had excused herself in order to get back to work. Long before this, Nick had pulled out his notebook and begun taking careful notes.

"LPOs?" he'd asked at one point, in response to something Paul had said.

"Limestone Pavement Orders. Local authorities issue them. Almost all the areas of limestone pavement in England now have LPOs on them."

"A bit like Tree Preservation Orders?" Nick knew about this aspect of planning control.

"Well, TPOs protect trees which may be fifty or a hundred years old. LPOs protect limestone pavement which is over three hundred million years old. But I suppose some people might think that they're similar."

"Are LPOs new?"

Paul shook his head. "1981 Wildlife and Countryside Act," he said. He paused. "I think you'll find that the powers are in Section 34," he added.

God, thought Nick, this man knew his trade.

It was as if Paul had read Nick's mind. He changed abruptly his manner. "Well, how can I try to explain? What you need to know is that the British Isles have some of the best limestone pavement areas in the world. Ireland has the most, a lot more than us, but Yorkshire and Cumbria have some great expanses as well. It's a unique habitat, but it's one that's been under threat. The problems began with the arrival of mechanical diggers. After the war, extraction of the stone started to happen on an industrial scale. By the 1970s, almost every bit of pavement in England had been damaged in one way or another. It was obvious that protection was needed."

"And LPOs have done the trick?"

"Well, they've helped. We know that illegal quarrying is still going on, though."

Nick's pencil had been racing over the pages of his shorthand notebook as Paul had been speaking, the half-finished ciabatta long left at the side of the plate. Now, back in the office, he flicked again through his notes, looking for what he needed. He turned back to the keyboard, and typed:

> Cumbria and Yorkshire have some of the best areas of limestone
> pavement in England. Originally formed hundreds of millions
> of years ago from coral and shells, the limestone was later
> scraped flat by glaciers during the Ice Ages, leaving the current
> distinctive flat platform areas criss-crossed with deep crevices.

Then he reached for the delete key. This was information which he would probably need to include somewhere in the piece, but further down the page. He couldn't assume he'd yet grabbed his readers' attention. He told himself to think journalistically. The question his readers would be asking was: Why is this story interesting?

It was funny how sometimes an article came together quickly, whereas on other occasions nothing seemed to come right and you could labour over it for ages. Nick had a hunch that the difficult news-pieces to write tended to be those where he had a personal interest in what he was writing. As, he had to admit, he now did in this story. He tried another approach.

> Extraction of the stone for landscaping purposes and for
> garden rockeries destroyed many unique stretches of limestone
> pavement in England before legal protection was introduced
> in the early 1980s. However, some garden centres continue to
> supply illegally extracted limestone pavement.

This still wasn't working. Nick sighed, and went back to his notebook.

Paul had been helpful but had been adamant about one thing: he couldn't be quoted. His council had a strict rule, he said: media approaches had to be made through the press office. Really, he wasn't sure that he ought to be meeting Nick at all, but still...

What Paul did give him were some contacts. As soon as Nick had got back in the office, he'd rung up an organisation called the Limestone Pavement Action Group. Yes, a helpful woman there told him, didn't he know, they'd been campaigning to raise public awareness about the issue for years. And yes, of course, she was happy to talk to the press. What did he want to know?

She'd confirmed what Paul had said, that it was against the law in England to remove limestone pavement – she used the term water-worn limestone. Well, normally against the law, she qualified herself. Apparently there were a handful of quarries down south where planning permission had been given years before. Things weren't quite so straightforward in Wales and Scotland, and there was a lot less protection for limestone pavement in Ireland, she said. It was a problem: it meant that sometimes stone merchants could pass off English limestone as coming in from Ireland.

"So it's not illegal to sell this stuff?" he asked her.

"No, only to dig it up. That's a weakness in the law."

"And there's money in it?"

"Yes, there's definitely money to be made. A few years ago we did a survey. Limestone was selling at up to £400 a tonne. We reckoned that the trade was worth well over a million pounds a year, perhaps significantly more."

"Where's it sold?"

"Stone merchants sometimes, and sometimes garden centres. Normally the stone is broken down and sold in small bits. People want small rocks and stones."

"Gardeners?"

"Gardeners for their rockeries, yes. Landscape designers, too."

"And what happens if you're caught taking a digger to a limestone pavement?"

"Well, you might get prosecuted. That would be only if the planning authority felt it had a strong enough case. And if you were found guilty, you'd get a fine. Maybe a few thousand for a first offence. There have been very few prosecutions, though."

"So, any advice to gardeners tempted to buy water-worn limestone?" Nick was angling for a quote he would be able to use in the piece.

"I just wish gardeners understood the destruction they inadvertently may be causing to some of England's most beautiful areas. It's perfectly possible to use other types of stone for your rockeries," she said. "Once a limestone pavement is removed, it's lost for ever. Millions of years of geological rock formation gone in an instant."

Perfect. Nick had already typed up her quote which was now on the screen in front of him, waiting like a soldier ready to be deployed where it was needed. He'd slot it in to his article in due course, once he'd got the first three or four paragraphs of the story completed to his satisfaction.

"Anyone else you think I should talk to?" he'd asked finally before ringing off. At her suggestion, he'd had a long call to a local naturalist, a man by the name of Robin Fakenham who was apparently something of a specialist in the flora of limestone pavement areas. Too much of a specialist. Nick had asked an innocent question about the sorts of plants which you could find, and Robin had launched into an extended monologue:

"Well, now let's see, there's a whole number of rare plants you can find, if you look carefully. There are Dark-Red Helleborine, they're not common, Bloody Crane's Bill, Angular Solomon's Seal, Herb Paris, Pale St John's Wort, Lesser Meadow Rue…" Once started, Robin Fakenham was hard to stop. "… Rigid Buckler Ferns, they're particularly associated with limestone pavements. Did I mention Mountain Avens, and Fingered Sedge, and…"

Nick had interrupted. "So what you're saying is that limestone pavement areas are home for some very special plants?"

"Absolutely. Limestone pavements provide shelter for many very rare plants not found elsewhere."

That was the quote which Nick had underlined, the one thing from his conversation which would make the final edit. Keep it simple. Sadly, this wasn't the week to tell readers of the *Cumbrian Enquirer* about the Angular Solomon's Seal, he decided. Molly would have laughed in his face if he'd dared try.

Chapter 19

Grizedale Forest comprises 5000 acres of commercial woodland covering the low fells east of Coniston Water. But it's also a tourist attraction, turned by the Forestry Commission into an outdoor playground for visitors. You can clamber twenty metres up into the trees and descend by zip wire, you can stroll along the footpaths and admire the outdoor sculptures, or you can get down and dirty on a mountain bike.

The press conference was taking place in a small timber and glass building which normally served as a centre for educational courses. Nick was late.

He'd gone down from home to Grasmere village first thing as he did every Friday to pick up his copy of the *Enquirer*, flicking through to see how the paper had come together. Not bad. The front page headline read Floods of Tears, which turned out to be a piece from Molly about the fact that some people made homeless from the terrible Cumbrian floods of recent years still hadn't been able to move back to their houses. His own limestone story was an inside page lead – page five again, he noticed.

He was back home, getting himself a cup of coffee, when the home phone tinkled. He strolled across to pick it up. Most of his friends tended to use his mobile, but he'd had a landline put in when he moved to Grasmere which he used chiefly for the internet connection.

"Good morning, Nick," said the voice. There was no introduction. "I'm one of your admirers. I read the *Enquirer* every week, and I particularly look out for the articles which you have written."

"Er – thank you." Nick was confused.

"Yes, indeed. You are, if I may say so, a very talented reporter. Your articles are always so readable. You seem so very well informed."

Nick didn't reply. There was something about the caller which didn't seem right.

"Now let's see," said the caller. "I was particularly interested in your article in today's paper on page five. And I was interested in the article last week, too, which was also on page five. And, goodness me, what a coincidence, the article the week before that. I expect you remember it. It was about a *dead runner*."

The line was momentarily silent. "And you know what I told myself? I said, that man Nick Potterton is working very hard writing all these articles. I said to myself, I think Nick Potterton needs to give himself a little break.

"Perhaps he should spend more time with that lovely girl-friend of his, spending his time running with her in beautiful parts of the Cumbrian countryside. Although perhaps he should also take care where he chooses to go running. Because sometimes it seems that they like to go running in very isolated places where, if an accident were to happen by some misfortune, it could be very serious."

Again the caller went silent. There could no longer be any ambiguity about the purpose of this call.

"And it would be such a shame if anything untoward were to *puncture* their happiness. Am I right?"

Nick thought quickly. "Well, thank you for your kind words and your thoughtfulness. Can I ask who is calling? I don't think you introduced yourself."

"Let's say that my name is Mr Atkinson."

"Mr Atkinson?"

"That's right: Mr Atkinson."

"Well, Mr Atkinson, I appreciate your call." Nick knew that he had heard the voice before but he had been struggling to work out where. He had just got it.

"Or may I call you Marcus?" he went on.

There was an audible intake of breathe at the other end of the phone. My advantage, Nick thought.

"Because, you know, Marcus, I've been keen to talk to you. I've got quite a lot of things I'd like to ask. When would be a good time to meet?"

There was silence, but the caller was still there.

"For example, it would be fascinating to know where the limestone pavement you acquire from poor Cumbrian hill-farmers ends up. Do you find it easier to sell to stone merchants or are there garden centres who are happy to accept the consignments? And another question, What do you –"

Nick realised that he had started to talk to thin air. The caller had hung up.

He sat down heavily on his sofa, and took a deep breath. In London, particularly when he'd been involved in investigative work, he'd ensured that his telephone number was ex-directory. When he'd moved north to Grasmere, there had no longer seemed any harm in appearing in the phone book. This was, after all, rural Cumbria, he told himself. Wrong decision: he was the only Potterton in the directory, a sitting duck. Davie's father had obviously tracked him down this way. And now Marcus also knew where he lived. Damn, damn.

It was irrational, he knew, but suddenly his home felt vulnerable. He hurried round, checking the window locks were in place and then putting a light on in his study upstairs. That would have to do for now: if he was going to get down to Grizedale he would need to leave immediately, he realised. He would have time when he got back to decide what to do next.

The road through Ambleside was unusually slow, and Nick then found himself behind a slow-moving farm vehicle for two or three miles near Skelwith Bridge. It meant that, by the time he arrived at Grizedale Forest, he had completely missed out on the initial coffee and biscuits and was ten minutes late for the formal part of the proceedings. The reception desk was no longer staffed, but he helped himself to the one remaining name badge, which read Molly Everett, *Cumbrian Enquirer*. He scrubbed out Molly's name, wrote his own name in, and picked up a press pack from the small pile which remained. The pack explained that the event was being staged to launch a new cycling strategy for the Lake District; after the presentations journalists were invited to stay on to try out for themselves one of the new mountain bike routes through the woods, and then there'd be a sandwich lunch available.

He made his way through to the main room and took a seat at the back. There were about fifteen people making up the audience. He did a quick assessment: a few journalists who like him worked for the local media, a few who were probably there representing the cycling press nationally, and then there were also a few odds-and-sods brought in no doubt to help swell the numbers. At the front, two people were sitting behind a table: Forestry Commission and county council, Nick guessed. And then there was a third person, standing up and half-way through a PowerPoint presentation.

Hadn't the world got tired of PowerPoint yet? Nick sighed, and settled down to listen.

The slide being projected read "Adventure Capital of the UK: the Lake District's cycling offer." The cycling offer! What sort of English was that? Who wrote this guff?

And then he recognised her. Oh god. The speaker was Pauline Peters.

Well, of course it would be Pauline Peters, he told himself, hadn't she told him that cycling was one of her responsibilities at Cumbria Tourism? Why hadn't he realised that she would be here?

Nick listened distractedly as Pauline described the details of what was being proposed. There was obviously some European grant funding which had been successfully tapped. His attention wandered. Would he have come if he had known Pauline Peters would be here too, he asked himself? Well, he was simply doing his job, and so was she. But, actually, no, he probably wouldn't have come, he decided. He would have given the invite back to Molly. The words of Pauline's father were still fresh in his head: he had, he recalled, been told to keep well away from the Peters family. In rather stronger terms than that.

Pauline was followed by the two other speakers, and after that three or four questions were asked from the floor. Nick had made a few notes distractedly, but was relieved when the session broke up. He left the room quickly, keen not to find himself next to Pauline.

Outside, a member of staff was allocating mountain bikes to the journalists, sorting out saddle heights and handing out cycling helmets. Nick hadn't necessarily intended to stay for this part of the event, but on the other hand he was feeling no great desire to get home. He allowed himself to be given a bike, and gathered with the other participants in a melee near the building.

"We're going to show you one of the new mountain bike routes we've just created." It was one of the other speakers talking to them. "It's an easy grade route, but obviously take care. The total is about four miles, but feel free to turn round at any time if you want. Maggie –" (a gesture to the woman who had been giving out the bikes) "– will be here all the time, and if you get back early you can help her put the sandwiches out."

The party set off. Nick decided to keep to himself at the back of the pack. He began to enjoy himself. Unlike some of his club mates at Coniston and Hawkshead, unlike Lindsay for example, he didn't do a great deal of cycling, but this was easy stuff, on a beaten earth path which was winding its way into the forest. He began to think of other things. He began to ponder whether he should report Marcus's call to the police.

"Hello, Nick." Another cyclist had slowed down to come up alongside him, and had begun talking to him. Nick looked up, and realised: Pauline Peters.

"I didn't know you were coming today," she said, slightly accusingly. "You weren't on the list."

"No, I'm here instead of my editor. I didn't know you'd be here, either. I'm conscious that I'm not the most popular person in the Peters family at the moment. In fact, I think I'm currently fucking off out of your lives, if I remember rightly."

"My dad. Mm, he does sometimes speak his mind."

"You can say that again."

Nick was silent. Pauline continued to ride alongside him.

"Can I ask you something?" she said. "I bought a copy of the *Enquirer* today, and you had an article in it. That article, was it – ? Was it indirectly about Davie?"

Nick didn't reply immediately.

"Yes, it was," he answered eventually.

"Thank you. I guessed it was. It's... It's good to know," she said.

Again they continued cycling. Pauline broke the silence. "There's something else I want to ask, if that's OK."

She got no further. There was a sudden call from a cyclist ahead of "watch out, there's a big hole here," and the next moment Nick felt his bike slip sideways. He struggled to control it, failed and as he fell, brushed against Pauline. She, too, fell.

"Oh, god, you alright?" Nick looked across at Pauline, who was lying on her side on the ground.

"Fine, I think. But no thanks to you. My dad was right. You're nothing but bad news."

"I'm really sorry."

She got up, and retrieved her bike. "OK, don't worry. But I'm going to push my bike back. You go on."

"I'll walk back too." Nick dusted himself down, and started wheeling his own bike, keeping pace with Pauline. "You were just about to ask me something."

"Yes… I was wondering whether you'd rung that number I gave you. The person called M. Was it Marcus? Do you know his address?"

"It's Marcus, but I'm afraid I don't know his surname. He's still pretending to be Mr Atkinson."

"Rowan Atkinson? I thought it was – er – the driver of the wagon who started that?"

"All sorts of people seem to call themselves Mr Atkinson at the moment. Why are you asking, though?"

"Just interested."

Nick had stopped, and turned to face her. "Pauline, you should be aware that Marcus phoned me today, after the *Enquirer* appeared. A threatening phone call. He's obviously aware that I know what he's been up to. So be careful. After all, Davie's death, we still don't know what happened. I don't think I told you that I spoke to Steve Miller, the runner who was leading the race at the Bad Step. Steve told me that he thought there was someone else up there on the mountain, hiding in the mist. He said he felt them back away as he approached."

Pauline had visibly turned white as Nick had mentioned this.

"No, Steve Miller must be wrong," she said. "I'm sure that there couldn't have been anyone there. I'm sure my brother slipped on the rocks."

They walked on in silence, pushing their bikes.

"Pauline, I am trying very hard to do as your father told me, but there's one more thing which I'd like to say. Your dad let slip that someone called Paddy Richards had been round to talk to your mother. I'm a journalist, I'm nosy, so I did an online search on the name the next time I was at work. There was a single press article from years back, about a loan shark with the same name. If it's the same guy and he's hassling your mother, she needs to get help. Tell her to go to the Citizen's Advice Bureau. Or even the police. Please."

Pauline didn't immediately reply.

Nick looked across: "Please tell your mother," he repeated.

Pauline looked back at Nick. "I'll mention what you say."

Chapter 20

The train from Euston pulled in to Oxenholme station shortly after one o'clock, and about twelve or fifteen people got off. Nick was waiting on the platform. Rosa, in chunky-knit jumper and leggings, and with a backpack over one shoulder, made for him and gave him an enormous hug. "Hello, dad," she said.

It was raining. It wasn't just raining, torrents of water were dropping vertically from out of an inky black sky. It was as though all the rain for weeks had been held in a plastic tarpaulin above their heads which someone had just come along and punctured.

"I see the weather's not changed since I was last here," Rosa said.

"Quick, make a dash for the car. It's just over there."

Inside, with water dripping from them on to the car seats and floor, father and daughter looked at each other. Nick leant across and gave Rosa a kiss on the cheek. "Welcome to the Lake District," he said.

They drove slowly back through Kendal and then took the main dual carriageway towards Windermere.

"I've got a really pleasant day planned for us on the hills," Nick said, as his wipers struggled to push aside the great gobs of water which were hitting the windscreen. How do you fancy the Kentmere horseshoe? Great views."

"What a lovely idea," Rosa replied. "Got any others as good as that?"

"You have to believe me, it's not always like this."

"Sometimes it's snowdrifts instead."

"OK, here's another idea. How about we find a pub, preferably one with a roaring fire, where we can settle down and have a meal?"

"That's an even better idea. But I want to pay."

"Why?"

"Because I feel like treating my old dad. Because the job's going well. And because I've got something to celebrate."

"What's that?"

"I'll tell you later," Rosa replied.

Nick turned off to take the road to Bowness. Normally he tended not to use the little ferry which plied back and forth across the waters of Windermere. It was a venerable Lakeland tradition dating back centuries, but it wasn't cheap and the queues of cars waiting to get on could be horrendous. However the ferry was the quickest way across to the pub which Nick had in mind for lunch. More a restaurant than a pub, really. Molly had taken him there once shortly after he'd started at the *Enquirer* for a getting-to-know-you lunch. He was sure it had log fires.

They were the only car on the ferry, and they were almost the only car in the pub car park. Inside, however, there was a pleasant buzz of conversation. About six groups were in, about ten or fifteen people in all, most of them sitting at dining tables and already half-way through their main courses.

"Restaurant table or comfy chairs in the bar?" Nick asked.

"Oh, let's do this properly. Restaurant," Rosa replied. "That table just next to the fire."

They settled down, steaming slightly as the warmth reached their damp clothes, and looked at the menu.

"I guess we've got plenty of time. I'm having a starter," Rosa said.

It was very comfortable being in Rosa's company. Nick didn't see enough of his daughter. The lovely child which he and Ana had brought into the world had turned into a fine young woman, strong and independent, and a delight to be with. He should arrange to meet her more often, he told himself.

"Here's to my talented father." Rosa was holding up the glass of dry white wine which she had ordered.

"Here's to my wonderful daughter," Nick replied, holding up his own glass. He'd ordered a dry white, too. Just the one, and then he'd switch to mineral water.

They slowly tackled the starters. Rosa has chosen grilled goat's cheese, which came served on a toasted slice of olive bread and with a home-made mango chutney. Nick had chosen the soup of the day, which was borscht.

"Careful not to spill that, beetroot stains are impossible to get rid of," Rosa said.

"Thanks. Just remind me, are you my daughter or my mother?"

Rosa laughed.

"So, Rosa, tell me everything. What are you doing? And what are you celebrating?"

Rosa put down her cutlery and looked across at Nick. "OK, dad. I hope this isn't going to be too much of a surprise. I want to invite you to my wedding."

Nick put his own spoon down.

"Your wedding? As in you and Becky?"

Rosa laughed. Her laugh, Nick thought, reminded him of her mother's, a large, warm Mediterranean laugh which reached out and embraced you in it.

"Dad!" she scolded him. "Of course I'm talking about Becky and me. What else could I be talking about?"

Nick took another sip of wine. Sometimes he felt his age. When he'd been Rosa's age, the friends he'd known who were gay and lesbian had often had to hide their relationships. Things were moving forward.

"We haven't got a date yet, but we're planning something for May or June. In London," Rosa went on.

She paused and looked across at Nick. "My mother will be coming," she said.

"Have you told her?" This was in a neutral tone.

"I phoned her a few days ago. And Becky and I plan to go out to Barcelona in a week or two's time."

"How is she? Your mother, I mean." Again, Nick was speaking neutrally.

"More Catalan by the day. When I phoned, she seemed to have to make an effort to switch to English. She answered "Digui?" and I said "Hi, it's me." And then she said, "Qui ets?" and I had to reply, "Sóc la Rosa, la teva filla!" Only then did she seem to get it."

Nick offered back a small smile.

"Dad, Jordi will be there for the wedding. He wants to come with Mum."

There was a pause. "OK," said Nick.

Rosa looked up at her father. "Dad, you have to accept it. I know you loved Mum, and she loved you too. And I know you both loved me, and you still do. And nothing will ever change those good times we had as a family. But life moves on. Mum's life has changed, and she's happy with Jordi. You need to be happy for them both."

"I know, I am really," Nick replied.

"I'm worried about you, you know. I'm worried about you up here, living by yourself miles from anywhere. Have you found anyone yet?"

Nick laughed. "Rosa, that's the sort of question that a parent asks their child, not the other way round! But since you ask, no, I haven't."

"What about the editor of your paper? Molly, isn't that her name? What about her?"

"Molly is a good colleague, but she has been happily married for at least twenty-five years to a solicitor in Cockermouth. It's a kind thought, though."

"OK, someone you run with then?"

"Yes, I've lots of friends in the club and one or two good friends. But let me try to put your mind at rest. I'm really very content with my life as it is at the moment."

"OK." Rosa sounded unconvinced. "But then there's your work, too. You used to be a national journalist, working for some of the best papers in the country, and now you're up here in Cumbria. Writing about – what did you tell me once was the term French journalists use for the boring everyday news stories?"

"Chiens écrasés. Squashed dogs," Nick replied.

"Squashed dogs. You're spending your life writing about squashed dogs."

"Not all the time. I mean, I've been working on quite an interesting story for the past few weeks."

"Tell me," Rosa replied.

"OK, well it started three weeks ago today, when I was doing the Bowfell fell race. Weather a bit like today, in fact." Nick briefly told Rosa the story. She grimaced as he described Davie's death, and then listened attentively as he relayed the developments in the weeks since then.

"So you think it wasn't an accident?" she asked eventually.

"I've been trying to piece it together and I'm not quite there yet. But, yes, I'm afraid I think it wasn't."

Nick looked across at Rosa. "What do you think?"

"I don't know. I think 95% of the time when there's something you can't immediately understand the answer turns out to be the most obvious explanation. Or, in this case, a straightforward fall. But on the other hand there's always that 5% of times when it isn't, when what actually happened in real life turns out to be so unbelievably unlikely that if you saw it in a film you'd think it was outrageously farfetched. Sorry, that's the best I can do."

The starters had been cleared away, and the main courses put in their place. Rosa had bangers and mash, which was to say a very posh version of bangers and mash comprising a good-looking Cumberland sausage curled around a creamy heap of potatoes. A tasty onion sauce completed her plate. Nick had chosen a fresh trout, farmed of course but organic, and from only a short distance away in the Eden valley.

"Una truita, mmm!" Rosa said, looking at the fish. "Do you remember that time when we were on holiday north of Barcelona and you ordered trout and got an omelette?" Catalan could be tricky: it used the same word for both.

Nick laughed. "I do, yes! That was a good holiday, wasn't it?"

"It was. So, dad, I was asking you about your work. And I was saying that I was worried."

"Well, as you said yourself, our lives change. I was fortunate to have the career I had in London, but there are other ways to make your life. Other worthwhile ways. That's what I've discovered."

He changed the subject. "My turn now: tell me what's happening in the world of commercial law."

They slowly finished their meals, and looked at the dessert menu. It was after half past two and almost all the other diners in the restaurant had left, but their waiter seemed unperturbed and happy for them to take their time. "The English cheese plate," Nick said. "Why don't we share that between us? And two coffees."

It was almost half past three when they eventually got back to Grasmere. The rain was as bad as ever and had lashed at them as they made the quick dash from restaurant to car and then from car to house.

"You're on the sofa-bed as usual, if that's OK" Nick said, as they both hurried inside to the warm. Rosa made her way up the stairs.

"Looks very tidy up here," she called down.

"Tidied specially," Nick responded, following her up.

"How's the book going?" Rosa was looking at Nick's files, which had been migrated from the sofa on to his desk.

"So-so. It looks like I've got a trip organised next month to the French nuclear site I want to visit. I'm trying to set up something for Finland for the new year."

"Finland?"

"A place called Olkiluoto on the west coast. The first new nuclear power station in western Europe, so something a landmark. There've been lots of problems with the development."

"You don't speak Finnish," Rosa observed.

"You're right. Bit thoughtless of your mother to be from Catalonia. If she'd been from Helsinki, I'd have had a head-start."

Rosa laughed. As she did, Nick's home telephone rang. He leaned across to his desk to pick it up.

"Hello?"

"Nick, it's Pauline Peters." There was a pause. "Sally left me a message earlier. To say that she was off to meet with Marcus." Another pause. "I've not been able to reach her since."

Nick took in the news.

"Do you want me to come and help?" he asked.

"I think I do," she replied.

Chapter 21

If you live in Cleator Moor, or indeed if you live anywhere in west Cumbria, it's best to accept that travel takes time. And if you decide to take the little rail service which runs round the coast from Carlisle down to Lancaster, it's advisable to be prepared for a very slow journey indeed.

From Whitehaven down to Barrow, just down the coast you might think, will take a good hour and a quarter. Carrying on round Morecambe Bay to journey's end in Lancaster will take another fifty minutes. Here are the railway stations that Lord Beeching forgot: tiny halts like Drigg and Silecroft and Foxfield where you have to flag down the driver as the train approaches if you want it to stop.

Sally took her car into Whitehaven in time for the 12.54pm train south. She'd thought to take a book, and she'd also got some food to eat – a sandwich, an apple and a chocolate bar. One of the problems, though, was that she didn't know how long she would be on the train.

She'd rung the number on the piece of paper she and Pauline had found in Davie's flat. M… Marcus, the person Davie had been working for in the weeks before his death.

She'd got the idea the afternoon she'd been round at Pauline's place, when the journalist from the local paper had turned up out of the blue and, after he'd left, she and Pauline had gone through Davie's text messages. It was pretty clear to them both that Marcus still owed Davie some money for whatever it was that he'd been doing. Quite a lot. That money would go nowhere near filling the great financial hole that Davie had left behind, but everything extra would help. Sally wasn't too concerned for herself, but she did want Pauline to get what help she could. Even so, it looked as though Pauline would have to sell her home and rent instead.

She hadn't mentioned her plans to Pauline. She had a feeling that Pauline would have insisted on coming too, and she wanted to do something to help her. She was very conscious of the fact that she'd let Pauline down in a big way a few weeks earlier. This would enable her to make it up.

Marcus had been cagey on the phone but in the end had agreed to meet up. He knew of her, he said. "Sally the sculptor," he said. "Davie told me about you." Sally hoped Davie hadn't said too much.

Marcus had rung back to her mobile with the arrangements. They'd meet on Saturday afternoon, he said. "Get the lunchtime train from Whitehaven," he'd told her. "Make sure you sit in one of the very first seats in the front of the train. I'm not quite sure what my plans are but I'll make sure I'm at one of the stations along the way. Look out for me."

"So where do I get the ticket to?" she'd asked.

"Oh, best get it all the way through to Lancaster."

It was unsatisfactorily vague, but it was at least an offer of a meeting. She did as arranged and took a window seat directly behind the driver's compartment, settling down with her book. The Cumbrian coast went past outside the window. The train reached St Bees, skirted the Sellafield complex, drew into Millom and continued down into Barrow-in-Furness. No-one arrived to meet her.

After Barrow, Sally began to have second thoughts. As each new station pulled up alongside the window, she scanned the platform anxiously for a stranger, there to meet her. The train called at Rouse: no-one approached her. Ulverston: still no-one.

Beyond here were quiet stations serving little more than villages. She pondered what she was doing, and didn't like the thoughts which were coming into her head. Maybe this hadn't been such a good idea: a remote and isolated platform miles from anywhere wasn't necessarily the best place for a rendezvous with a man she'd never met and didn't know. It was prudent, she realised, to phone Pauline to let her know what she was up to.

It was a quarter to three when she phoned. It was the voicemail she got. Sally left a message, explaining what she was doing and adding that she would text through the name of the station where she was met. Always assuming, she thought after the text had been sent, that she could get a signal there.

The train continued. There were only a handful of stations left before Lancaster. The carriage suddenly seemed to be getting cold. Sally shivered.

Pauline had spent Saturday lunchtime shopping in Kendal. Her mother's birthday was coming up, and she wanted to get something special this year. Her mum needed cheering up at the moment. She got back to her house about twenty past three, feeling worried: her mobile phone wasn't in its usual place in her bag and she'd had a horrible feeling that she might have lost it somewhere about town. What a drag: she'd have to contact the network company and get a stop put on her phone. Which meant that she had to find the emergency number to ring. Where had she put that? God, what was happening to her these days? Why was she becoming so disorganised?

She took the shopping into the kitchen and put the bags down on the floor. Thank god, there it was – sitting on her kitchen table, with the charger still plugged in. Of course, she remembered now, she'd been charging up the battery just before she'd left. She picked the phone up idly.

There was a text message which had come in just a few moments earlier and she clicked through to read it. It was from Sally, she saw, but she couldn't make any sense of it at all. It bore the single word 'car'. Oh well, Sally must have sent it by mistake. Pauline deleted it.

And then Pauline noticed that there was also a voicemail awaiting her. She listened to it with mounting concern. How could Sally have been so rash? How could she have gone off alone to meet Marcus? Didn't she know that he'd already made a threatening call to the *Enquirer* journalist? Didn't she know...?

No, Pauline realised with a start – Sally didn't know. It was only because Nick had happened to be at the press conference the day before that Pauline herself knew. And then only because she had asked him about his article in the paper. Sally almost certainly wouldn't have got that week's *Enquirer* or, if she had, she wouldn't have put two and two together. She probably thought Davie had been doing nothing more than a legitimate delivery drop for a local company.

Pauline immediately tried to phone Sally back. Her own call went unanswered.

What now? Sally had said in her voice message that the train had just left Kents Bank. OK, so that meant that she could have been met at Grange, at Lancaster or at one of the three stations in between. And then – what? Pauline thought back to the text message she had deleted: the one word 'car'. And then bundled into a car and taken anywhere at all.

She thought of ringing her parents at their home but realised that they had driven up to Carlisle for an afternoon's foray round the shops. She tried her dad's mobile, but that went through to a voicemail. No point in trying her mum's mobile: this had been bought four years ago and had since spent almost all its life in a drawer in the living room. "It's for emergencies," Pauline's mother had said. Fat use that was – this could an emergency.

Should she ring the police? She didn't really want to: how could she explain the background, who Sally was, why she was meeting Marcus, why Pauline was worried? Who else was there who knew what was going on? Well, there was always the journalist. Hmm. It might not be a good idea, but it was all she could think of. She looked up Potterton in the phone directory.

The weather had been filthy for the drive back from the restaurant to Grasmere, but now if anything it was worse. As soon as he had taken the call from Pauline, Nick had left Rosa to sort herself out and had immediately turned the car around. The road was beginning to flood near Rydal and again beyond Windermere: basically streams were coming down off the hillside above the road and sweeping across the tarmac. If the rain continued much longer, there could be real flooding problems. Oh no, poor Cumbria, not again.

He forced himself to drive carefully, but the miles to Kendal dragged by. It was only twenty-five minutes but seemed like two hours when he finally turned for the third time into Pauline's street. No need to find somewhere to park this time: Pauline was waiting at her door, and rushed out as soon as she saw him approach.

"What do we do?" she said.

"Have you tried ringing Sally again?"

"Every few minutes. It's always the voicemail message. I think the phone's switched off."

"OK, here's my suggestion. There are five railway stations we need to check out. If we don't find her at any of those, we ring 999."

"Where first?"

"It'll be quicker to take the M6 now we're so near it."

"Straight down to Lancaster?"

"No, I'll come off at junction 35 and we can check Carnforth. Then go on to Lancaster. And then work our way back: Silverdale and Arnside and Grange."

Nick hurriedly did a three-point turn and pointed the car out of Kendal towards the motorway. The clock on his dashboard showed the time: 3.58.

Sally had stopped reading her book well before the train arrived at Grange-over-Sands. The train was running ten minutes late: it had already turned three o'clock. She couldn't concentrate. She pondered leaving the train at Grange, and waiting for one back to Barrow and Whitehaven. On the other hand, she'd already come so far. She suspected Marcus wasn't going to show. She'd get to Lancaster, have a bite to eat at the station café, and then work things out. It might be better to get a fast train to Penrith and then get a bus from there back to Whitehaven. A wasted day, though.

A few people emerged from the shelter at Grange station and hurried to get into the carriage. No-one approached her.

Normally the train journey from here onwards would be a delight. Close to Grange, the railway line runs along the very edge of Morecambe Sands before turning to cross the water on the fifty brick pillars which together hold up the Kent viaduct. But Sally could see nothing from her window but driving rain. She was surprised when the train slowed to a halt at Arnside station, signifying that the viaduct had already been crossed. She peered out on to the platform. No-one waiting for her.

It was a similar story five minutes later at Silverdale. Sally looked at her watch: already ten past three. Fifteen minutes to go to Lancaster.

Shortly after 3.15 the train made its penultimate stop, at Carnforth station. The automatic doors opened and a few people got in. One man turned to approach her.

God, this was it. She hurriedly began typing a text message, got the first three letters down and then realised that her predictive text would never cope with the whole word Carnforth. No time. She hurriedly sent off what she'd typed. Pauline would have to work it out.

"Hello, Sally," the man had reached her. "I do hope you've enjoyed a pleasant journey. This is where you get off."

Chapter 22

"What could be more appropriate than the Carnforth station refreshment room for a man to have a meeting with a woman? And such an attractive young woman."

He was sitting across the table from Sally. There was a pot of tea, a milk jug, a hot water jug and two cups and saucers between them, as well as a plate bearing cakes. English afternoon tea.

There were other people about. It was probably a good sign that Marcus had chosen to meet her somewhere like this, Sally thought. Perhaps her concerns were unfounded.

On the other hand, when they had first sat down he had very firmly reached across for her mobile phone which she had put on the table, switching it off. "A curse of the modern age. It's so discourteous if a phone rings when you're meeting someone, don't you agree?" He ostentatiously made to turn off his own phone. She had wanted to complain at his presumption, but she had been taken by surprise by his action. He had a confidence, or perhaps an arrogance, which was difficult to confront.

"Have you seen the film?" He was talking to her again. "Of course, it was based on a play by Noel Coward. Quite daring for its day."

He meant Brief Encounter. It could hardly have been anything else. Carnforth station, in its bustling heyday and under the alias of Milford Junction, was the backdrop to the iconic David Lean film, the tale of two strangers who meet by chance, fall in love, and then part. The film appeared in 1945, at the very end of the war. Today Carnforth station is a shrine to the film's memory, a museum for a movie, attracting visitors from around the world. And they come especially to see the refreshment room, where the lovers first meet and where they meet again for the last time at the film's end.

"I have often thought that the film must have captured the spirit of that wartime period. The danger, the uncertainty, and the romances that blossomed. The sexual opportunities. What do you think? Do you think Celia Johnson should have left her suburban husband and allowed herself some excitement in her life?"

It appeared to be a question which didn't require an answer. He went on speaking.

"Of course, in the film Celia Johnson is just about to make love to Trevor Howard when someone comes back to the borrowed flat they're using and disturbs them. Not so much coitus interruptus, more coitus not-even-begunus." He laughed at his little joke. "But the Noel Coward play is more ambiguous. Perhaps they did get it together after all."

He paused. "What would you have done, Sally?"

"I'm afraid I don't know the film," Sally replied. It was not quite true. She had seen it once, a few years back, in a black and white season held at the Ambleside cinema.

He was probably in his thirties, Sally thought, looking at him. She had found her gaze drawn against her will to his hand each time he reached for his tea cup. The fourth finger of his right hand bore an enormous signet ring, dominating the whole hand. It complemented a large gold ring which was wrapped around the middle finger of his left hand. Beyond the wrist of the right hand was a gold bracelet. Beyond the left wrist was a watch. It looked like a Rolex.

He was wearing a blue silk suit which could perhaps have looked sharp on the right body. Sally thought it just looked tacky. A white shirt bulged round a nascent paunch; higher up, the collar struggled to get itself safely round his large neck. The top button of the shirt was undone behind the tie, Sally noticed. The tie itself was a curious confection. Surely not some sort of regimental affair? Sally pondered its provenance as Marcus continued talking. Probably Lancashire Cricket Club, she eventually decided.

"Love and death, so closely related," he was continuing. "At the film's end, Celia Johnson nearly kills herself. Under the wheels of the speeding express train. Well, not Celia Johnson, her character of course. Laura. Those famous lines she speaks: *I really meant to do it. I stood there trembling right on the edge, but I couldn't.* It's a powerful scene. *I had no thoughts at all, only an overwhelming desire not to feel anything ever again.* Have you ever had that feeling, Sally?"

"I'm sorry, as I said I don't know the film." Sally knew she had to drag the conversation back to her own agenda. "I'm here just to talk to you about Davie Peters. I know he worked for you."

"Davie, yes. Oh how insensitive of me to talk about death like that. It must have been a terrible shock to you. So sudden."

"I believe you still owe him his wages. I hope I can trust on your honesty not to renege on what you owe."

"Of course you can trust me. But – forgive me for mentioning it – what precisely is your interest here? I know you were Davie's girlfriend. But he told me that you had chucked him. He was very upset. He told me how much he had loved you. And he told me other things too. You left him a very bitter man."

The hand reached down the cup again. "Of course, you're very good looking, Sally, and I expect you have lovers queuing up all the time. But Davie was a nice lad. I can't understand why you gave him up."

"I'm sorry, but I'm not here to talk about my relationship with Davie. How much was due to him when he died?"

"You see, my problem is that I'm not sure I can tell you. You weren't married to him, you weren't family, you weren't even his girlfriend at the end. Some people might think you're asking for confidential information here."

"All right, Marcus, I quite understand. I'm sorry to have wasted your time." Sally made to get up from the table.

"No, please sit down." It was more of a command than a request. "I'm sure we can sort this out."

He reached in to the inside pocket of his jacket and pulled out a large leather wallet. He opened it, pulled out three bank notes and pushed them across the table to Sally. "There you are," he said.

"Thirty pounds! Is that it?" Sally was astonished. This was not what the text messages implied at all.

"Well, just between ourselves I've rounded it up. But I won't ask you for the change."

Sally left the money where it lay. She said nothing. She felt a fury she could not articulate.

"Don't forget your tea, it's getting cold," the man continued. "Listen, let me float an idea past you. I don't know how you're off for money but I imagine that, like most of us, you could always do with a little more. I was happy to give Davie some work, and I'd be happy to do the same for you. I've got various business interests, including a couple of clubs I own down in Morecambe and Blackpool. Gentlemen's clubs, you know, pretty girls and so on, but absolutely legit. Licences from the council, all that. I'm sure I could use your own particular talents."

Sally took in what he was saying and, without even pausing to think, reached across the table and slapped him hard across the face. As she did so, she was conscious that two men who had been sitting in a far corner of the refreshment room came rushing up.

There was silence for a very long moment. So Marcus had come with backup support. The men looked at him expectantly, waiting for a response. Sally waited too, barely breathing.

He finally spoke. "All right lads, no problem here," he said.

"Oh dear, you've got me completely wrong," he went on, making what could pass for a smile in Sally's direction. "What on earth did you think I meant? No, I was talking about the sculptures you do. I try to have a few choice pieces of contemporary art in the clubs, it helps create the right ambience."

He reached down and pulled out something from a case he had at his feet. "I admire your work. I wondered if you could do me a few more pieces like this one," he said.

He had pulled out a slate sculpture of a Herdwick sheep. It was the sculpture she'd made a year back, which she had awarded to a sweaty Davie Peters after a local fell race and for which he'd given her a kiss on the cheek. His first kiss.

"How did you get that?" she asked.

"Well, after you chucked Davie, he obviously didn't want this any more in his flat. Bad memories. So I bought it off him. Fifty pounds, was that fair?"

"I'm buying it back," Sally said. She reached into her own purse, and pulled out the three remaining twenty pound notes which were there. She slapped them down on the table next to the three ten pounds, picked up the sculpture and rushed to the corner of the room where there was a black rubbish bin. She cracked the slate against the edge, and allowed the broken pieces to fall inside. And then she left the room, rushing out to the platform. A train was just coming in, going south. She jumped on, not caring where she ended up.

Nick and Pauline had faced driving rain all the way down the M6 from the Kendal junction to the Carnforth turn-off. Nick pulled in to the station and Pauline immediately jumped out. It was a little after a quarter past four.

The station was deserted. A sign on the refreshment room door said that it closed at four, and the little exhibition centre devoted to Brief Encounter was closed too. The station was back to performing its role as a branch line stop serving a small town.

"Any sign of Sally?" Nick called across. Pauline came back, shaking her head. "No, and nobody to ask either. It's like a ghost station."

She clambered back into the car.

"Lancaster then?" Nick said.

"Lancaster it is," Pauline replied. "And then we try the other stations."

Nick turned the car round and headed back to the M6. One more junction south and then the road in to the town centre and a wriggle through to the station. Half past four. The heavy rain clouds meant that it was already getting dark.

They found Sally sitting alone on a bench on the station platform. She looked utterly exhausted. She looked up as Pauline and Nick approached, smiled wanly, gave Pauline an enormous hug, then looked questioningly at Nick. It was the first time they had met face to face.

"I'm Nick," he said. "We've – spoken briefly on the phone. And – you once sent me a text."

Sally looked at Pauline.

"It's all right now," Pauline said.

And Sally burst into tears.

Chapter 23

Nick had intended to ring first thing on Monday morning, but in the end Molly had waylaid him to talk through some of the stories for the forthcoming week's edition. He finally got to the telephone about quarter past ten.

"Hello, George," he said, as the phone was answered.

He had decided on Saturday evening that he would make this call. Time to put Detective Inspector Mulholland in the picture about Marcus and his activities, he thought. He'd floated the idea as he had driven Pauline and Sally back up the M6 on the way back to Pauline's house in Kendal where Pauline had arranged that Sally would stay the night. Picking up the car could wait till daylight, she'd said.

But Pauline hadn't been at all keen at Nick's suggestion. "Don't get the police involved," she'd said. Of course, Nick realised, she must be worried sick that Davie's role would come to light – and her father would certainly not welcome yet another encounter with the detective. A little to Nick's surprise, given what had happened that afternoon, Sally had supported Pauline.

But, when he'd talked it through over breakfast on Sunday morning with Rosa, she had encouraged him. "Bring in the professionals," she'd said. "Just in case this is one of those 5% occasions and there really was some funny business up at the Bad Step." She was busy packing her bag ready for the train back south. Her new walking boots that she had brought with her remained pristine. They would have to wait for another visit.

George Mulholland had immediately recognised Nick's voice on the phone. "How nice to hear you, old boy," he said. He was his usual affable self.

"Short notice, I know, but I was wondering whether you were free at lunch today, George?" Nick asked.

"A pleasure. Perhaps a little early in the day for us to start your initiation into the misty splendours of the island of Islay, but a jar of Cumberland bitter might be in order, I think."

"I need to talk to you about the Davie Peters affair," Nick said.

"Well, what a strange coincidence," George Mulholland replied. "I have just been talking about Davie Peters myself."

"Really?"

"Yes. I've just had a telephone conversation with the coroner."

"The coroner?"

"Yes. It's all sorted out. He's releasing the body today to the family, and has signed the death certificate."

"Right." Nick was absorbing this information. "So what has he decided?"

"Oh, it's what we were all anticipating all along," George Mulholland responded.

"It's what we were anticipating?" Nick echoed.

"Yes. Accidental death, of course."

Chapter 24

The little church of St Olaf's stands alone in the fields at Wasdale Head, sheltering among the trees in the green valley below England's highest mountain. It was packed. Nick had failed to get anywhere near the church, or even the church door, and was in a crush of people squashed into the small churchyard. It was a beautiful location. Great Gable was there ahead, a fabulous mountain, and beside it Kirk Fell. Yewbarrow closed off the valley to the west. The Scafell plateau was away up to their east. The deep dark waters of Wast Water lay still and silent a short distance to the south. A beautiful place to be, and such a beautiful day too. It was glorious, as autumnal days sometimes could be in the Lakes. A low sun was shining down, illuminating the dark greys and greens of the hillsides. It was the first Saturday in November, and the rain of the weekend before seemed a lifetime away. The sky was blue.

Lindsay was beside him in the churchyard, and so too was almost the full membership of the Coniston and Hawkshead Harriers. Not just his own club, either. He noticed faces around him he recognised: Ambleside, Cumberland Fell Runners, Helm Hill, Keswick, Kendal, Borrowdale, all the other Lake District running clubs had turned out.

The crowd had spilled out even beyond the churchyard. A little way away on the path heading back to the Wasdale Head Inn Nick spied a familiar mop of black hair: Steve Miller must have driven up specially to be here. Pennie was beside him, and talking to the two of them was another familiar face: of course, it was Jim Henderson. He would have come up from Sheffield.

Lindsay nudged Nick and pointed in the other direction. He followed her gaze. Standing a little apart, quietly and modestly, was an older man. "Look who it is," Lindsay said. The man, a retired shepherd who lived not far down the valley, was a living legend in fell-running circles where his exploits had remained unmatched. Even by Davie.

So many runners together. It was like the start of a fell race. In fact, Nick realised, exactly four weeks earlier many of the people here today would have been lining up with him just across the hills in Langdale, looking forward to a great Lakeland race, wearing their club vests. And Davie there too, amongst them all, of course. Just a month ago.

Someone had rigged up a rough-and-ready loudspeaker system outside the church, but little of the service happening inside came through to Nick and the others around him. He heard odd snatches. At one point a familiar Biblical phrase carried to where he was standing: *I will lift up mine eyes unto the hills.* Nick did as instructed. Over beyond Kirk Fell a buzzard was gliding gently in the air currents. A shaft of sunlight momentarily lit up the summit behind. What a wonderful country.

There was no coffin in the church. Davie's parents had arranged a quiet funeral a few days earlier at the crematorium near Workington. It had been a family-only affair, close family and Sally, or so Nick had gathered. Instead Davie's friends had been invited for the memorial service here at the Wasdale Head chapel where, if you believe the stories, the roof beams had come straight from Viking longboats. Later on, everyone would be foregathering in the lounge of the Wasdale Head Inn.

First, though, there was a final tribute to be paid to Davie's life. As the service finished and the church congregation started spilling out, there was a rapid flurry of activity. Like most of those around him Nick had come prepared, just needing to take off a layer or two of clothing to reveal the running clothes he had been wearing underneath. Fast runners were invited to make their way to the summit of Great Gable the long way round, up past Sty Head. Everyone else who wanted could jog or walk their way up the more direct path above Gable Beck, to the col beside Kirk Fell and then up the stiff little climb to the top of the mountain. Nick and Lindsay chose this latter option.

Half an hour or so later, both groups had joined up once again. A mass of runners and walkers congregated on Great Gable. And there, in the early afternoon of a perfect autumnal day, a handful of Davie Peters' ashes were scattered to the four winds of Cumbria.

Nick waited until most of the crowd had started the descent before making a move. He wanted a little time to reflect and to be with his own thoughts. As he began to start picking his way carefully back off the mountain, he realised that he had been joined by a companion.

"I wanted to talk," Pauline said. "I wanted to thank you for the article you wrote about Davie."

"Thank you," Nick replied simply. His feature had appeared in the previous day's paper. He had given it his very best effort. He had painted the picture of a young man who relished his life and who adored the mountains. He had described Davie's achievements, both as a schoolboy and an adult. He had hinted at the fulfilment which could be found in running over the hills. He had included tributes from other runners, and from those who knew him as a friend. He had even managed, against all the odds, to work in one of the quotes he had been given by Davie's old head teacher Anthony Richardson when he had interviewed him almost a month earlier in the bungalow outside Keswick.

He had said nothing in the story about the other side to Davie's life which had come to light.

The article was illustrated with the photograph Pauline had lent him: Davie, young, fit, happy, at the moment of winning a race. He and Molly had pondered long and hard the headline to choose. They had nearly gone with *The runner whose luck ran out*, but in the end had felt that this was altogether too cheerless. Instead they had together agreed on the replacement. The two-page spread on Davie Peters now had a simple but effective title: *The man who loved the fells*.

"It was kind of you not to go into any more of the detail. You know, about the background," Pauline said.

"Well, it wouldn't have been appropriate in the circumstances. After all, we know what the coroner found. It was accidental death."

Nick stopped briefly to look at the view. Spread below him was the valley of Wasdale and the waters of the lake beyond. Pauline stopped too.

"Did you ever doubt that – ever think that it might not have been an accident, I mean?" Pauline asked him.

"Well, Davie had certainly got himself mixed up with some interesting company," Nick replied. He paused. "I spoke to Mulholland again a couple of days ago, and they're going to keep an eye on Marcus. But Mulholland didn't seem very interested in what I told him about the limestone. I got the impression that our geological heritage is a pretty low priority if you're a detective trying to keep the country crime-free. I suppose the council may try to prosecute the farmer in due course, if they think they can get a conviction. If so, it'll be a fine and a couple of paragraphs for me on an inside news page."

"But you suggested to me that day at Grizedale Forest that Marcus could have wanted to kill Davie."

"I toyed with the thought, and I wanted to get your reaction. But it was never clear to me what he would have gained from that. Why risk such a high-profile crime? And he didn't sound like the sort of person who would have been happy clambering about a misty hillside waiting for a runner to come past, or even getting other people to clamber around on his behalf. I don't think Marcus is a man of the mountains. Blackpool Tower, that's probably as high as he gets."

"He really did owe Davie quite a lot of money, judging from Davie's text messages. Several weeks of trips with that limestone."

"Yes, but you'll have to accept that you'll never get it off Marcus now. And I'm afraid you'll never get back the money Davie spent in the last few months. He was borrowing off you, wasn't he?"

"He'd borrowed quite a bit from Sally, but he'd taken quite a lot more of my money. I was stupid, I suppose, but he was my kid brother and I loved him dearly. And the money all went, just like that."

"He was gambling?" Nick asked.

"All the time. Online. I think it was blackjack. He seemed to have a group of people he played with regularly online. They must have loved it when he logged on."

She paused.

"He'd had a big win earlier in the year. A thousand, I think. And you know how Davie was – always a risk-taker, always wanting to push himself to be a winner."

"And this time, in the end, he lost." Nick responded. "By the way, is your family still being pestered by that loan shark? Paddy Richards."

"I persuaded my mother to go to the Citizen's Advice Bureau. Like you suggested." Pauline seemed to be gazing down to the valley bottom, way below. "Mum wasn't at all keen, but in the end she plucked up the courage. The people there told her the contract she'd signed was completely unenforceable. They wanted her to go to the police, but you know what my parents are like. Instead the CAB are arranging for a solicitor's letter to be sent to Richards, and they say that should almost certainly be the last we'll hear of him."

"I suspect Paddy Richards will barely even be bothered. Unfortunately, he has plenty of other people to prey on, people who won't think to get advice when they get into money problems."

There was a long silence between them.

"You know, this is the moment where you can turn the page and put the past few weeks behind you, Pauline. A clean sheet," Nick said.

"Maybe. But there hasn't been time yet. We had such a terrible long wait for the coroner's verdict."

"Yes, that's true. And I suppose that as long as his enquiry was going on, there was always a sliver of doubt. That perhaps it wasn't an accident."

"Yes," Pauline agreed.

"You must have been worried."

"Yes," she replied again. "I was."

"Because there was always the fear there that perhaps the coroner would decide that there really was someone up at the Bad Step waiting for Davie."

"I suppose so."

"Always the anxiety that the coroner would call for an inquest. That the police would open a formal investigation."

"Maybe," she replied. "Yes."

"Although if there had been someone at the Bad Step waiting for Davie, it would have to have been someone who knew the mountains as well as he did. Someone quite prepared to wander round the back of the Crinkle Crags in thick cloud and heavy rain. Someone who knew that Davie was running the race, and what time he'd be arriving at the Bad Step. There are not many people who'd meet that person spec, I'd say."

"No," Pauline agreed.

"I mean, off-hand I can only think of one person who would fit the bill."

"Yes?"

"The only person who comes to mind is you, Pauline."

Pauline said nothing.

"Fortunately, it's all hypothetical now. The coroner has finished his inquiry, the police have moved on, and my feature on your brother is completed and published. That's all past history, and that's the way it has to remain. But I would still be interested to ask you a question, hypothetically speaking of course. Could you tell me what happened at the Bad Step that afternoon?"

There was a very long silence between them. Pauline looked down towards Wast Water, and then very slowly turned to face Nick. Everyone else was already far down the mountainside. They had been left alone.

"In hindsight it was a completely crazy idea," she said at last. "But you have to realise that we were desperate. The last few weeks had been a nightmare. Davie had refused to talk to either me or Sally. He wouldn't answer the phone, and he wouldn't answer the door. And he was burning up money all the time."

She stopped talking momentarily, to order her thoughts.

"Sally and I decided we had to do something. We had to get him to confront the mess he was making of his life, but we knew he'd never agree to meet us voluntarily. And the only thing we could think of was that he would be running the Bowfell race. We knew he'd be leading it, or very near the front. So it seemed the solution."

She paused, and then continued. "Sally and I arranged that we'd go up to the Crinkle Crags together. We chose the squeeze point just above the Bad Step. We decided we'd lock our arms together, make him stop and listen to us.

"Well, as you know, it was terrible weather. Sally... Sally really didn't fancy being out in a thunderstorm. Afterwards, I know she felt really guilty that she'd left me in the lurch. She thought that if she'd been there, things could have been different and maybe she was right. Or maybe not. Anyway, I went by myself. I took the car to Wrynose Pass and came up from the other side. It was easy – I know those fells backwards.

"I nearly accosted the first runner who came past but just managed to hide myself again in time. Davie wasn't far behind. I stood right by the Bad Step, and I told him we had to talk."

Pauline was silent.

"So? What did he say?" Nick prompted her.

"I told you that the whole idea was crazy. He told me to get out of the way. He said he was in the middle of a really important race, and that I could be stopping him from being English champion. He barged past. He – he may have called me a bitch. His own sister. And then, I don't know what happened, but I think we had a tussle. A bit of pushing and shoving. I've thought about it again and again in my mind, but everything happened so quickly. I don't know. Perhaps I pushed him over the edge?" Pauline stopped, and then continued quietly. "Perhaps I murdered Davie?"

She stopped. A gentle breeze had got up from the direction of Yewbarrow.

"It was terrible. I had to get back down to my car. I had to pretend when my parents phoned later that I knew nothing. And everything that happened after that – going to the mortuary, and having to sort out Davie's affairs, and Sally blaming herself for not being there too, and then people like you barging in all the time. And all the dealings with the coroner."

They carried on slowly down the mountainside, and approached the main bridleway back to Wasdale Head.

Pauline looked at Nick sharply: "How did you know I was there?" she asked.

"Well, I did say that I was only asking you a hypothetical question, Pauline. But I suppose I could have picked up a few clues over the last month which, had I wanted, could have led me to a hypothesis like that. I suppose I could have mulled over something you said to me the very first time we met, for example, when you said how awful it was to see Davie looking like he did in his running kit. I could have mulled over what you could have meant, given that in the hospital mortuary he would have been in a hospital gown. And, after that, I could have pondered to myself who could possibly have been the apparition that Steve Miller told me he saw at the Bad Step. And I could have come to a conclusion."

Nick paused briefly. "But now that the coroner has given his verdict, I guess my hypothesis has to be ruled out."

Pauline looked at him. "What do you mean by that?"

"Well, I don't doubt that sometimes coroners do make mistakes and sometimes, perhaps, they think that deaths were accidental when they weren't. But in this instance, what I tell myself is that the coroner has got it right, even if perhaps not for the right reasons. Whatever happened at the Bad Step, whether you pushed or whether you didn't, it was still an accident."

They had lost height quickly, and were nearly back to the valley bottom. Ahead was the inn, where the lounge was already packed to capacity. The wake was about to get under way. The sun was beginning to disappear behind the western fells. They walked back in silence.

Afterword

It was another Monday morning at the *Cumbrian Enquirer*, and Molly was smoking another fag.

"Nick," she said cheerfully as she saw him arrive. "All ready for another busy week, I hope."

Newspapers were ephemeral things. You worked on a story, wrote it, and then moved on. In less than four days, another issue of the paper would need to be at the printers, full of new stories, new news. Put the past behind you, concentrate on the present.

"Ready and willing," Nick replied. "What have you got for me?"

Molly pulled together a sheaf of papers. "There's lots come in already. Let's see. There was a bit of a problem at a firework display down in Millom at the weekend – some rubbish caught fire, I'm afraid. I'd like you to deal with that. Then we have the county council budget problems. Could seem boring, but actually very important of course. There's a tourist who claims to have seen a ghost at a hotel in Keswick, or so he claims. Wants his B&B money back, cheeky monkey."

Molly pulled another piece of paper from the pile. "But I want you to get started with this one. It's a bit sad: a faithful old sheepdog at a farm over in Borrowdale who got run over on Sunday. A speeding motorist who didn't even stop."

She looked up: "As you'd expect, the family are devastated. It wasn't just a working dog, it was a family pet," she concluded.

Nick reached for his notebook. "OK, Molly," he said. "I'm ready to make a start. Give me all the details you've got."

Also available from Gritstone Publishing

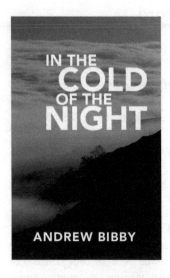

In the Cold of the Night, by Andrew Bibby

The staff at Greensleeves residential park are undertaking the Three Peaks Challenge for charity. But their attempt to climb the highest peaks in Scotland, England and Wales in one weekend goes badly wrong. As they begin the walk up Scafell Pike in the Lake District their boss disappears. Next day his half-naked body is found in a moorland bog, miles off route.

As the police begin their enquiry Nick Potterton, once a successful London journalist but now a struggling part-time freelance for the local press, also investigates. The 'Body in the Bog' story becomes the paper's front page lead and it falls to Nick to try to find out exactly how Richard Meade met his death.